Accidental Virgin

A Novel by
James A. Costa Jr.
and
Frances R. Schmidt

CCB Publishing
British Columbia, Canada

Accidental Virgin

Copyright ©2025 by James A. Costa Jr.
ISBN-13 978-1-77143-615-1
First Edition

Library and Archives Canada Cataloguing in Publication
Title: Accidental virgin / by James A. Costa Jr. and Frances R. Schmidt.
Names: Costa Jr., James A., 1931-, Schmidt, Frances R.
ISBN 978-1-77143-615-1 (pbk) – ISBN 978-1-77143-616-8 (PDF)
Additional cataloguing data available from Library and Archives Canada

Cover artwork: ID 41499962 © Syda Productions | Dreamstime.com

Publisher: CCB Publishing
              British Columbia, Canada
              www.ccbpublishing.com

Introduction

Carly Miller and I, Bryan Perri, invite you, dear reader, to hear the story of our relationship told from our individual points of view. It begins about ten years ago in a cemetery, a most unlikely place for romance to be born, progresses to a friendly restaurant and a number of locations along the way.

The story is sometimes humorous and often tumultuous as we deal with our emotions and life experiences and the conflicts resulting from them. Can love survive where secret fears compound our already problematic relationship? To learn the answer, we invite you to share our personal drama in *Accidental Virgin.*

Chapter 1

While squatting beside my father's monument in Buffalo's Forest Lawn Cemetery, and running my fingers over his name chiseled into the polished marble, my thoughts turned inward, seeing again his sharp blue eyes darkened by disappointment. I could still see the grim set of his doctor's jaw in his final days, the same way it was when he had to impart bad news to a patient. It was my fault. Having me, his only son, follow in his footsteps was his dream, as if only that could complete his life, as if only that mattered, and everything else counted for nothing.

I remembered the closeness of my youth, the warmth and love that marked our relationship until my college years when I rejected medicine as a profession. Then came, the arguments, the insults and bitter recriminations that wore us down:

"Son, you have the ability, the talent, the brains. And money's no object. Don't you see the golden opportunity you're throwing away?"

"But I don't have the heart for it, Dad. Don't you understand? Or the stomach for it. How many ways can I say it? Medicine's not for me. It's just not!"

"Bryan, listen to me," he pleaded. "I can open doors for you, ensure you a secure future, give you prestige in the community. Someday you'll have a family. You'll want the best for them, too."

It was hard to stand up to my father, a man of strong will, a good man, a good father, but I had to fight back for the sake of my own manhood, my independence. As much as I wanted to please him, I had my own life to live and I intended to live it my way, even though I wasn't yet sure what it might be.

Arguments erupted from time to time, followed by long silences and my mother's hand-wringing nervousness. Finally came my father's brooding resignation and withdrawal that left him forever saddened, grievously wounded, like a man mourning some great loss, as I stood now, mourning at my father's grave, not only for the father I lost, but for something that had been lost between us several years before his sudden death.

I straightened up, hurting with regret and guilt I doubted time could ever completely heal. How insignificant our differences seemed to me now, how trivial the endless arguments now that my father was gone. I uttered a few silent words I prayed my father could somehow hear and understand. As I raised my head, the sun parted the billowy white October clouds and warmed my face.

That's when my eyes fell on her for the first time. She was standing some forty feet distant near the peninsular edge of the cemetery lot, her head bowed and her hands buried in the voracious pockets of her beige, knee-length jacket. She might have been an angel, sculpted like the statuary surrounding her, or a beatific vision, with the sunlight radiant on her face, and her dark hair blowing free from the sides of her turned-up collar.

Or was she merely a ghost, an apparition? Intrigued, I stood a long time watching her, entranced by this solitary figure in this most solitary place. I felt oddly drawn to her, as if something tangible were flowing between us, although she seemed totally unaware of my presence.

I stooped to retrieve the trowel I had used to clean up the weeds around my father's granite stone and tapped the dirt crumbles from it. When I rose she was gone. I glanced about, looking every which way, over the swales and grassy mounds topped with several marble and sandstone mausoleums. I peered around several rows of headstones and monuments, stood on tiptoes, saw no one. My heart fell. Was I hallucinating? Impossible. I know I saw a woman, a real woman, a woman as real to me in those scant moments as I myself standing there. I felt agitated. I lingered, shaking my head, scanning the area again. Mystified, I wondered if being in that sad and lonesome place had addled my senses.

A gust of wind skirling across the rainbow-carpeted earth lifted a billowing cloud of fallen leaves like a flock of startled birds. Reluctantly, I turned and headed back to my car, my head low, my feet crunching the coarse gravel covering the lane.

I dropped the trowel on the floor behind my car seat, and moved to climb in when I saw the sunlight glint off the tail lights of another car, mostly hidden by foliage on a separate lane just around the bend. Could it be? My spirits picked up. I knew now I wasn't hallucinating or going mad. As I approached, I saw her standing there in a beige jacket and blue jeans, looking lost and lovely. I hurried toward her. Sensing her apprehension at my approach, I assumed what I thought was my most disarming smile.

"Car trouble?" I asked in as pleasant a voice as I could muster.

She backed up a step. "Of sorts, I guess."

"If your battery's dead, this is the right place for it," I punned, instantly worried that my little joke might be in bad taste, though not as bad as my original thought: *What's a nice ghoul like you doing in a place like this?*

In that moment our eyes met before wavering in mutual uncertainty, I thought I saw the twitch of a reassuring smile. She

3

edged back. "The battery's fine, I think. I—"

"Must be your choke, then. Two to one that's the answer. Common problem with these pre-fuel-injected models. Do you have a hood latch inside?" I asked, stripping off my top coat and laying it over her open car door.

"No, but—"

"No, of course you probably wouldn't in an older model like this. *Secretly I wondered where she found an old clunker like this one.* I'll check it out for you," I said, moving around to the front of the car. "I'm no expert, understand, but I've tinkered a lot with car engines in automotive class in high school, so I do know quite a bit, if I say so myself." Finding the latch inside the grill, I lifted the hood while keeping up a steady stream of light banter to keep her from thinking or worrying too much about my possible motives.

"You're lucky you don't have a broken fuel line or something like that, at least not as far as I can see. These wires are getting pretty brittle, though. They could use a changing," I said, hoping to impress her. "Better have them checked out the next time you take it in for service."

I stole flickering glances at her as I spoke. Up close she looked even more dazzling than she did from a distance. Uncovered now, her hair, raven black, hinted at mysteries unplumbed, especially the way it partially shielded her face and unfurled to her shoulders.

"Wow, take a look at the gunk on this engine, will you? It's a wonder this baby ever started up at all. Or didn't actually catch fire. I've seen it happen once before, on my first car, in fact. Just like that, in an instant, the heat of the engine ignited all the gummy stuff. I was afraid it would hit the gasoline vapors and blow the car to pieces. And me with it."

"Oh, my gosh," she said, peeking under the hood tentatively

and stepping back again.

"I have an old blanket to cover the fender—to keep me from getting greasy while I work. Nothing upset my mother more than having to wash greasy clothes, but I'm sure you know how that story goes. Anyway, that moth-eaten blanket came in handy for smothering the flames before anything disastrous happened. It was literally a life saver. You better make it a point to get the engine steam-cleaned, too, when you take it in, and make sure they check the head gasket."

"I certainly appreciate your advice, but—"

"Don't worry, it's free," I chuckled, soaking up in furtive glances the flashing blue eyes that seemed to take in everything and nothing at once, the delicate chin tucked in defensively, the fine, slender nose with nostrils slightly flared, like a forest creature testing the air for danger. The tilt of her head suggested a wariness and —what both scared and excited me— a certain sense of danger or, at the least, adventure.

I lifted the greasy cover and stuck my finger into the carburetor throat. "Do you want to try starting it now?"

"I really doubt—"

"We won't know till we try, will we?" I said, amused that she, a woman, should presume to know more about cars than I did. "I think this will fix it," I said, mightily pleased with myself. Smiling, I watched her from the corner of my eye, trying to gauge my effect on her.

"Look here first," I instructed, cleaning my fingers with a tissue from my pocket and motioning her close. "If this ever happens again when you're alone, just stick a pencil or something like it right there." I gestured. "That'll hold the choke open while you turn the key to start up." Judging by her wide-eyed expression, I knew I was impressing her. "Once the engine fires up, take the pencil out, set this cover back on and screw it down tight with this wing nut. Simple as ABC," I added, noticing the frown spoil her smooth brow. "Now if you want to get in and start—"

"I'm sure it's valuable to know all that," she offered hesitantly, and before I could interrupt her again, she said, "but I believe the problem is there."

Puzzled, I followed her pointing finger toward the battery. "But you said it wasn't dead."

She poked downward. "The tire," she said flatly. "It's flat."

I know my face turned beet red and I stepped back, running my hand through the mop of hair flopping over my damp forehead. *What a jerk! Of all times to make a fool of myself. A major fool!*

"I noticed the lean of the car," I said, stammering, "but…but I thought she was just on a low shoulder here."

"Yes, I can understand that."

"You can see it's on a little downhill slope here, too."

"Yes, I see it is."

What did that tiny smile at the corner of her mouth mean? Or was it a smirk?

"And with the body so low to the ground, it's really hard, even under the best of conditions to tell the tire's flat."

"Yes, I see that. It is hard to tell, isn't it? Lucky, I just happened to notice it when I approached that side of the car. I probably would have ruined the tire if I tried to drive away on it."

I bent down and inspected the wheel. "Uh-oh. This tire's shot, totally. Split in the sidewall. Wouldn't have made any difference if you did drive on it." I straightened up. "You're fortunate it didn't blow while you were moving on the highway, otherwise you'd have lost complete control and...well...."

She shuddered. "I see what you mean."

"I'll change it for you," I said, covering the carburetor, screwing it down and slamming the hood. "You do have a spare, don't you?"

"Yes, but I don't think—"

"Don't tell me, let me guess: the tire's fine but you don't have a jack. It never fails. It's okay, though, I have one in my car that will work."

She brightened. "Oh, yes, yes, I do have one."

"Well, that's a plus," I said, rambling on compulsively, hoping to keep her mind off the embarrassment still burning my wounded ego.

The lavender scent of her perfume wafted on the breeze made me giddy as I took her keys and moved to the rear of the car. I raised the trunk lid and stooped inside.

A loud thunnkk reverberated from the compartment as the lid dropped suddenly and struck my head. Dazed, I reemerged, blinking hard and rubbing my crown. "Looks like you have a faulty piston there, or something," I said, smiling foolishly trying to ward off another round of embarrassment.

Instinctively she moved toward me. "I'm sorry, I really am. I should have warned you about that. I forgot all about it. I've been meaning to have it fixed. Are you all right?"

It hurt a lot but I said, "It sounded worse than it was." I touched my head and looked at my fingers. "See?" I said, holding them up, "no blood. Which is good because I hate the sight of blood."

Seeing for the first time her open, unabashed, dazzling white smile dissolved my insides and jellied my knees. I wondered, is this what's called 'love at first sight'?

"A minor concussion, maybe," I joked, "but nothing to worry about." I braced the lid and reached in for the tire. "Uh oh, problem. Sorry to say, but it looks like this one's flat, too."

She drew in her neck, sheepishly. "Yes, I thought it would be. That's what I've been trying to tell you, but…"

'But,' yeah, but he'd been so damn busy jabbering away she couldn't get a word in edgewise. I knew what she was thinking.

"…but you surprised me … appearing out of nowhere, and everything happening so fast—well, I just couldn't quite get anything out."

Well that was kind of her to say. At least she tried to spare my feelings. That stood in my favor.

"I hate cars," she blurted, wringing her slender fingers and frowning at the rusty blue heap.

I noticed the several rings on her fingers, but no wedding band. A good sign, but I didn't like the way her lips tightened and her face darkened.

"It's all right," I said. "Everybody has car trouble from time to time, even with new cars. It happens to the best of us, usually when we least expect it. This may not be the worst possible time, but it couldn't be a worse possible place. At least we still have daylight." I handed over her keys. "Come on, we'll take it and have it fixed. Then I'll bring you back and change it for you."

She seemed to shake herself free from whatever she was thinking. "Really, it's nice of you to offer, but if you'd just have someone come out from a garage… I don't mind waiting."

"They may not show. You know how dependable people are

these days?" *These days!* I said it as if I were an old man of fifty-eight years instead of twenty-eight.

"If they know my situation... if you tell them, I'm sure someone will come."

"Don't count on it."

She drew herself up suddenly. "I'll manage. Thanks anyway."

I didn't quite understand. Did she fear me? Why would she trust some stranger from a garage to come and help, and not trust me? Was she telling me to get lost, that she didn't like *me?* Did something about me turn her off? Or did she really believe she was putting me out?

I chose to believe the latter. "It's no problem for me. I have nothing but time, right now, anyway."

She tucked her hands into her jacket pockets and cocked her head at an angle that caught the afternoon light in a way that accented her high cheekbones. In the pooling blue of her downcast eyes I sensed a haunting that belied the smooth serenity of her face.

"I don't have my cell phone," she said. "Do you have one I could use?"

"My battery's dead...oops."

She smiled. "I have a friend," she began hesitantly, "so if you just drop me off near a phone I'd appreciate it. That much I can accept."

A friend? A 'he' friend? "That'd be silly, wouldn't it?" I pressed. "By the time your friend gets here— if he can even find the spot— the gates are likely to be chained. It gets dark pretty early this time of year. Think of it, your poor car here, all alone, waiting for you to come back." I gestured with a grand

9

sweep of my arm. "How would you feel being locked in a cemetery all night? In the dark. All by yourself."

A glimmer of a smile parted her lips. "I don't think I'd care for it, thank you."

"Good, neither would I and neither would your car. It's creepy enough in the daytime. Unlock your trunk again and I'll pull my car up."

She hesitated. "All right."

I grabbed my coat off the open door and strode away, unable to believe my luck. A little time, just an hour or so, is all I ask. But I had to be careful. No more blunders or I'd lose her for sure. Let her do the talking, I reminded myself, people love the sound of their own voices. Don't try to be clever. Let her see me as a safe, solid, salt-of-the-earth kind of guy.

Looking back, I saw her in profile, gazing toward the spot where I'd first seen her. Against the backdrop of swaying, half-naked trees, black under milky-blue skies, of gravestones lifting gray heads from quilted blankets of reds and yellows and browns, amid showering swirls of autumn leaves blowing on fitful gusts of wind that tugged and plucked at her hair, she stood there, shoulders drawn together, looking wistful and forlorn, like Christina in an Andrew Wyeth painting, mysterious and remote.

I pulled up behind her car and climbed out. "I know a gas station about a mile from here over on Amherst Street. We can have coffee in the restaurant next door while it's being fixed. Get the chill out of our bones."

Guarding my head against another ambush, I held the lid up with one arm as I dragged the tire out of the trunk and lugged it to my car. "Shouldn't take long to fix it, unless they're busy." I prayed they would be.

She balked, looking around apprehensively. "Are you sure about this? I really don't—"

"We have to get it done and get back before they padlock the place." He extended his hand. "By the way, I'm Bryan."

Her fingers barely touched his. "I'm Carly."

"Okay, Carly, let's go."

God, she was sitting beside me. In *my* car. A little too far over, for sure, almost against the door, but there, and scared to death, too, if her demeanor meant anything: knees vise-tight, arms locked across her chest, eyes riveted on the road ahead. I sensed an iron will beneath that delicate facade.

Not until we hit the boulevard did she seem to relax a bit. I even managed to draw a couple of smiles from her as I worked up a small sweat trying to win her confidence. She seemed to breathe freely for the first time when we pulled into the station.

Chapter 2

I felt relieved when we pulled into the service station. This smiling Good Samaritan seemed nice enough and safe enough, but you never could tell about a person. Sometimes the ones that seem the nicest are the worst. Now that we were near other people I felt safe.

"An hour and a half. At least," the greasy young attendant muttered through a cloud of cigarette smoke.

"That long?" I asked, feeling disappointed.

"Hey, lady, I only got two hands, okay?" He snapped away his cigarette butt and hefted the tire from the trunk of Bryan's car. "I'm supposed to been done half hour ago." He scowled toward two truck tires waiting for repair.

Bryan looked pleased, like he won a prize or something.

We left the station, cut across the lot and parked in front of the Italian Garden, a small brick-faced restaurant next door. The sound of soft music and the sweet smell of sauces and warm bread greeted us as we stepped inside.

Bryan said, "It's a little dark, but I think it's open." He touched my arm. "How about sitting over there?"

We threaded our way between empty tables crowded together and covered with red linen tablecloths, and headed toward a more secluded one along the side wall. A shaggy gray head poked through a pass-through window in the rear. "Be right with you folks."

Bryan took advantage of the moment to excuse himself to go wash his hands. He returned a few seconds before the old man shuffled up to our table.

"Dinner we don't serve for another hour, folks, but if you want something light…."

He stood slightly stoop-shouldered, with his hands folded over his aproned pot belly. "Some nice minestrone or chicken soup? A sandwich, maybe, I make it special for you. Meatball, capicola…." His gray mustache did a little dance and he smiled benignly from face to face. "Italian sausage?"

"I'll just have coffee," I said.

"The same for me, please."

"This your first time here?" the old man asked, reaching to light the candle between us.

"Not for me," Bryan said, "but if I remember right, this used to be a donut and coffee shop."

"Right." The old man clapped his hands together. "Now I got it, my wife and me. Four months ago we bought it. We're still building it up, the business, but it takes time, like everything. Later, when the ball gets rolling good, anything you want all day long you can have. The whole menu, except breakfast. For that you go to McDonald's."

His eyes twinkled as he laughed and called over his shoulder, "Caterina, two café."

Bryan and I exchanged quick glances as he dragged a chair up to the table.

"Cream?"

"Please," I said.

"Not for me."

"Cream," he called, then rattled off something in Italian. "My name is Sam Contini," he said, offering his hand. "'At'sa my wife back there, Caterina. Without her it takes four women

13

to run the kitchen. Still she finds time to bake our own bread, Sicilian style."

"I'm Bryan Perri."

Sam cocked a shaggy eyebrow. "Italiano?"

"Half."

"And I'm Carly…Carly Miller."

Sam took her hand and patted it. "'At'sa different name— Carly. A pretty name. A pretty face, too. Like Carly Simon, the singer, eh?"

I'm sure I blushed. "You've heard of her?"

"Oh sure," he said, pursing his lips, leaning back and helping his ankle over his knee. "Britney, too, Madonna, Lady Gaga, Taylor Swift. I'm not so old I can't appreciate it, music, all kinds. I love it. Even some of your rock music."

"I like soft rock," I said.

"'At'sa far as I go, too. The other kind, 'at'sa not music. Makes my ears cry." Sam swung around and pointed to the music box with its colorful lights in the far corner. "A Wurlitzer. When's the last time you seen anything so beautiful like that? Almost like Sophia Loren, the movie star when she was young and beautiful."

"Only in the old movies on TCM," I said.

"Sure, only in the movies, like Sophia. You're too young to remember, both of you. But joosta in time, right after the big war, I come to this country. Thank God for that," he said, clasping his hands and rolling his eyes up. "Anyway, 'at'sa my machine and my records, my kind of music from my own collection. All from the Forties, most of it, anyway. Some from the Thirties. The big bands. Ahh, 'at'sa when music was music."

I noticed Bryan drumming the table lightly. He obviously was annoyed with Sam, for whatever reason I can only guess.

"Caterina, she's making the coffee fresh. It's almost ready." He glanced to each of us. "You know the old time big bands, any of them? Tommy Dorsey, his brother Jimmy, maybe? Benny Goodman, Duke Ellington?"

"Benny Goodman," I said, "and Glen Miller. My grandpa used to play their records."

"Miller, like your name, Miller, sure." He laughed. "*String of Pearls... In the Mood...* What a band! *Little Brown Jug.*" He clucked his tongue and shook his head. "He died missing in action, a plane crash, you know, in the big war."

I said I didn't know.

"Oh, yeah, he did. But his music, that will never die. Words I don't know too good, but music, ahh, 'at'sa in my blood. My Caterina and me, the way we used to dance, you wouldn't believe it. Any time a big band came town, we went, kicking up our heels. Everybody watching. We got trophies, even, to prove it, at home, in the china cabinet... What days!" He sighed. "Now I'm too old and Katie's legs can't hold up like before. Arthur-itis. So what're you gonna do, 'at'sa life. But still, at least, we can listen and enjoy."

"You're lucky," I said. "You have beautiful memories to treasure."

Sam gazed warmly at me. "Thank you, we do. Our kids, sometimes they make fun of us, but at least they could take it or leave it, our music, Caterina's and mine. Our grandson, Bobby, though, he's different. His ear is the same like tin." He hunched his shoulders. "Eh, what're you gonna do."

"Your grandson?" I asked. "Does he work in the business with you?"

15

"Him? Bobby? Never. He's a school boy, college. Nineteen years old."

I guess I looked surprised because he said, "Oh, you think we're too old to raise a boy still in school?" He laughed. "To tell the truth," he hunched his thin shoulders, "we took him in, Caterina and me, when he was five. But 'at'sa long story I'll tell you about sometime maybe."

Interested, I leaned forward, wanting to hear more. "What's his major?" I asked. "What's he taking up?"

"'At'sa what I ask him, 'What're you taking up, time and space?'" He laughed and shrugged again. "All he says is he wants to be a poet. Can you beat that? I tell him, 'Who do you think you are, Dante's Inferno?' But he just laughs when I say that."

I leaned back and folded my hands. "He's probably a very sensitive person."

"Oh, yeah, he's sensitive all right. I aska him how much money is that gonna bring in writing pomes, then he gets mad. He tells me money, 'at'sa not so important like doing what you love. I guess he's a got a point I can't argue too much with but I do anyway because it's okay for a kid, but you gotta grow up sometime and pay the bills. Money don't grow on trees." He sighed and shook himself as if from a reverie. "Look, let me play you something I bet you never heard." Hauling himself to his feet, he shuffled over to the juke box.

"Likes to talk, doesn't he?" Bryan whispered to me across the table.

I didn't like Bryan's tone of voice. "I think he's very interesting."

"Oh, I agree, I agree. I mean, you know, he doesn't let up."

"I don't see why he should. He obviously likes people. If we had more people like him the world would be a better place."

"Oh, no doubt, no doubt about it. I'm only saying some people would be put off by someone who... who invites himself in like that."

"Those are the ignorant ones," I said. My remark seemed to wither him. I turned and smiled at Sam's approach.

"Listen to this," Sam said, as the strings started in. "Harry James." He sat down heavily. "Like the others, he's dead now, too."

"I don't think—"

Sam held up his hand. "The trumpet, hear how sweet it comes in? Not yet... listen, listen... there." He tilted his head back and closed his eyes. "Where do you hear anything so beautiful like that anymore, I ask you, tell me where? Except maybe when you die and go to heaven."

"It is beautiful," I said. "What's the name of it?"

"*Cherry*. It's one hardly anybody knows, even before in the old days, nobody knew."

"It's very pretty. Quite romantic, too, don't you think so, Bryan?"

"Huh, oh, yes," he gushed, as if suddenly resurrected, "romantic, I agree, very romantic."

"My music," Sam said, "my music and my place." He leaned forward and clasped his hands. "This restaurant, I tell you the truth, it was Caterina's idea. Me, I'm a retired laborer. A construction engineer, if you want the fancy name. Local 211. If not for Caterina, I'd be home watching TV or maybe playing my accordion. Not like Art Van Damme, if you know who he is, but maybe a little bit like Dick Contino, if you know him, which I doubt, too. Or Lawrence Welk. He's dead now, maybe thirty years ago, but it's like yesterday. His name is almost like mine— Contino, I mean. He died maybe two or three years ago. Sam Contini, 'at'sa me; Dick Contino, 'at'sa him.

"All her life she wants to open up a place, my Caterina, nothing too big or fancy, mind you, so that you gotta depend on strangers who rob you, and then I said why not, what the hell— 'scusa my language. At first, to tell the truth, I was against it, her legs, you know, and my old age, not to mention it's taking a gamble. Money, we don't need, my pension, 'atsa 'nough, and everybody knows a restaurant, how mucha headache to run. Then I was thinking, even though we're getting up in the years— I'm eighty-five, almost eighty-six—come here from the Old country when I'm maybe fourteen, fifteen, sixteen, I can't remember no more. Can't speak English except maybe a—"

"You don't look eighty-five."

"Thank you, Carly. I feel good. Thank you very much. Still, I am. Maybe working all them years with the wheelbarrow and cement— Anyway, I'm eighty-five and Caterina's eighty-three, but don't tell her I told you or she'll brain me. Then one night I'm thinking, this is her dream. So I aska myself, why can't she have it? Our kids, all married with their own kids now, they're against the idea. They think we're crazy. 'You're old people,' they said. 'You can't do it.' All except the young one, Bobby, still in school to be who knows what, maybe another Shake-a-speare— he says, 'Go ahead, Papa, try it if it's Grandma's dream.' He's the only one on our side. The others, they are yelling at us to forget it. I said, 'What're you afraid we'll lose the investment and there goes the inheritance?' So after that they shut up their mouth.

"And now Caterina's got her dream. Maybe it won't work out and maybe it will. So far we hold our own okay. If you love something, you go after it, I say. Take a risk. 'At'sa what counts. Or else go lay down in the corner where it's safe like a dog until you die. At least this way you know you tried. What else can you do? Life, 'at'sa not like a stove or something you buy at Sears with a guarantee it's gonna work out and be okay."

"It sounds a lot like what your grandson is trying to do," I said, unsure if I should have said it.

Sam scratched the bald spot on his head. "You know, I didn't think of it that same way before. Maybe you got a point. I gotta think about it. Anyway, for me, music was my dream, to play in a band, a big band. But did I take a chance? No. I had a wife and kids, so I stayed on construction. So here I am, but I'm okay. Caterina's dream is my dream now, too. I'm a cook and waiter and washa the bottles, too. I like it. This whole thing…" he waved his arm, "…everything you see, 'at'sa her idea. But the jukebox, ah, 'at'sa my idea. Notice it don't take no money. Beautiful music, it should be free to hear for everybody."

"Sally!"

"Sal, Salvatore, 'at'sa me, but everybody calls me Sam. Only to Caterina, to her I'm 'Sally,' except when she's mad and I can't tell you what that is." He scraped back his chair. "Coming."

"What a nice man. I think his wife's a very lucky woman."

"It would seem so," Bryan said, looking at his watch.

Bryan looked a little agitated to me. "I definitely think so. Did you hear how he put his wife and family before his own ambition? Now that's a real man."

"If that's the way it really was."

Bryan was beginning to annoy me with his negativity. "What do you mean?"

"Well," he said, drawing himself up, "maybe he didn't have enough talent. Or he was afraid of failure. Who knows, it could be almost anything."

"You're rather cynical, aren't you?" I said, noticing he was getting a little sweaty around the neck.

"Not really. But it's my experience that the truth isn't usually on the surface. You have to dig a little to find it."

"Now that is cynical."

I saw his jaw harden and his shoulders tighten. I felt sure he was about to get combative, when Sam came carrying a tray.

"Coffee here," he announced, raising a cup with a flourish and placing it before me, "and over here, with cream on the side."

Bryan and I were a little bewildered when Sam lifted a huge bowl and placed it between us.

"Antipasto," he declared proudly, "by Caterina. Compliments of the house." A container sprouting foot-long breadsticks clunked down next, and last, two wine goblets partially filled. "My own," he proclaimed, stepping back and clasping his hands. "You try it. I think you like it."

Bryan started to speak, but Sam raised his hands. "Please, it gives me pleasure. Now eat. Enjoy. Maybe sometime you come back and try Caterina's specialty, veal parmigiana." He kissed his fingertips, then opened them like a flower to the sunshine of his smile. "Prima. The best."

After Sam faded gracefully away, Bryan said, "Shall we?" He took the huge wooden fork and spoon from the bowl. "Your plate, madam."

"Thank you, sir."

Elbows high, he scooped a generous portion onto my plate, then loaded his own.

I dribbled the oil and vinegar sparingly over my salad. "Isn't this a nice surprise? I'm so glad we came here."

"And to think, we owe it all to your flat tire," Bryan said, poking around until he finally found a plump black olive to start with.

I'm not used to apologizing, but I said, "I'm sorry, I shouldn't have made that remark."

Bryan looked at me, wide-eyed. "What remark?"

I knew he knew darn well what remark, and was still smarting from the sting of it. "Calling you a cynic. Implying you don't trust people."

"Oh, because of what I said about Sam? I didn't take it that way at all. It's a matter of opinion. Different strokes for different folks. You have your point of view, I have mine." He smiled. "I happen to prefer mine."

I put my fork down. "Oh? Pardon me!"

"Sure. Nobody likes to admit weakness. That's how I see it, anyway. Rather than change our ways or pursue our goals, we make up stories to justify our failures or shortcomings. After a while we believe our own lies. It helps us to accept ourselves, maybe even helps us to like ourselves. It's a defense mechanism. It's human nature."

"In other words" I said, "it's a case of seeing the glass half full or half empty. The pessimist versus the optimist."

"In other words," he said, "it's a case of seeing a glass that may not be there at all."

I stared at him, beginning not to like him very much. "That doesn't make sense."

"In other words," he said, "we're talking self-delusion."

"Are you saying that only your point of view is valid?"

"I didn't say that. I'm speaking generally. If you want to take Sam's words at face value, you can. It's your right. I'm sure he's a decent guy, sincere, honest, all the rest. But I don't believe everything I hear."

Even though Bryan softened his tone, I couldn't help bristling at his remarks. I picked up my fork and stabbed at my salad. "And I do?"

Sam's head poked through the kitchen pass-through window in the rear. "Hey, folks, listen to this one, *I Can't Get Started with You.* Bunny Berrigan on trumpet."

Bryan seemed relieved by the intrusion and threw him a salute. "Nice tune, isn't it," he said, digging into his salad. "Catchy. What did he say the name was, 'I Can't Get Started'? It's different, anyway."

Still feeling a little annoyed and a bit snarky, I asked, "Besides being a philosopher, you're not by chance into police work, are you? If you don't mind my asking, that is?"

Ignoring my barb, he glanced down to his blue suit and tie, a little surprised. "Do I look like a cop?"

I couldn't help squirming a little as I scrutinized him a long moment. I avoided his eyes, but managed to take in everything else, from his silver-blue tie to the heavy gold ring on his right hand. "You could pass for one."

"Actually, I'm a... an insurance investigator."

"Oh?" I think a twitchy little smile lifted the corner of my mouth. "Well, they're similar, aren't they?"

I thought he was being evasive, for some reason when he said, "Are they?"

"I think so," I said, trying to hold back a coy smile. "They see the worst in people." I don't mean that in a negative sense, of course. I suppose it is necessary in your line of work."

"And you think I'm like that?"

I pronged a piece of cheese. "I think you think like that."

He gave me a broad smile . "Well I think you think the way you'd like to think I think." Then he snatched a couple of breadsticks from the bowl and pressed one in my hand. "If it's a fight you want, let's settle it with a duel." He rose half-way up from his chair, brandishing his breadstick like a sword. "En guard."

I tapped his weapon away. "Maybe another time," I said, all flustered.

He persisted. Our sticks clashed and crumbled on the table.

Despite trying to keep my lips tight, I couldn't help smiling. Then the absurdity of it all made us both laugh. Quietly at first, then louder until we had the other customers looking at us like we were crazy. We finally grew embarrassed at our own silliness and forced ourselves to stop.

"Hey, you lovebirds," Sam called, "listen to this one, the HiLos' *Love Is Just around the Corner.*"

In the flickering shadow light, I couldn't tell if he was blushing. My own face felt hot. "Now that was silly," I said, dabbing the corners of my eyes trying to restore my dignity. "And I'm still not sure what you said makes any sense at all."

"Hardly anything I do or did, does. And let's not play with 'do or did does!'"

"Honestly," I wouldn't touch that line with a ten-foot bread stick."

"Touché," he said, filling his dish for the last time and drenching it with oil. "So, now that you know the kind of ogre I am, what do you do?"

I lifted my cup toward him. "I'm a waitress," I said, looking him straight in the eye. "At the Four Seasons." I could see by his surprised look that he didn't expect my answer.

"Which Four Seasons? Where at?"

"Across from the university. I attend school there. It's very convenient." I really seemed to have aroused his curiosity.

"Interesting. What are you taking up?"

"I hope not time and space like Sam says his grandson does. I have a degree in sociology, but I'm going for a Masters in Education. I want to teach."

His eyes widened at the revelation. "Great. I think you'll make a terrific teacher."

"Really?" I thought I'd put him on the spot. "Why?"

"Well," he said, straightening up, "you're... you're articulate... you seem to care about others... you're obviously intelligent—"

He made me smile. "That's enough. I'd love to let you go on, but tell me, what exactly *do* you do?"

He cut away the seeds from a hot pepper. "People have accidents. I check them out." He made a claw of his hand. "I look for negligence."

"Oh, stop it," I said, waving my paper napkin at him.

"I get police reports, statements from witnesses— that sort of thing."

I sipped my coffee. "It sounds interesting."

"Getting out and around is what I like because it gets me out of the office for a while. This afternoon I had to see a lady at St.

Vincent's parish, so, being in the area, I made a trip to the cemetery. That's why I happened to be there. I like to see that everything's okay, clean up around and make sure there's no vandalism. Like that." To my questioning eyes, he said, "My father."

I looked away. "I'm sorry."

"It's okay. It's been four years..... Well," he said, looking around and changing the subject, "they don't seem too busy." He pushed his plate aside and checked his watch.

"No waitress, either. Maybe they're slow because it's Monday."

He shook his head doubtfully. "Shall we make a toast?"

I picked up my glass. "What shall we toast to?"

"Listen to this one," Sam called through the window. "Harry James playing *You Made Me Love You.*"

Bryan raised his glass to mine. "To Harry James?"

Our glasses chimed a sweet note. "To Harry James."

After we sipped our wine, we lowered our glasses and fell silent. Listening to the mellow music seemed to wash away the vestiges of our earlier abrasions.

You made me love you... I wondered, was the song speaking for us?

I didn't want to do it...

I didn't want to do it.

You made me want you,

And all the time you knew it,

I guess you always knew it....

The song ended, breaking a kind of spell that momentarily seemed to fall between us.

"It should be time," I said, drawing back.

It looked like Bryan wanted to stay. I thought he was about to reach out and take my hand but then he pulled his hand away to reach into his pocket.

Brusquely, Sam waved away Bryan's money. "Next time you pay. And always remember," Sam said, "music, 'at'sa true language of love."

We thanked Sam and promised to come back soon.

It was raining when we left the restaurant. We ducked our heads and scurried over the rough parking lot. Bryan reached over and this time he did take my hand. His grip was firm and warm and we clasped fingers for a few seconds before I snatched my hand away. I don't know why I did that, but I remember the surprised look on Bryan's face. Or was it a hurt look? We acted as if nothing happened as we climbed into his car.

After driving over to the station to pick up the tire, we headed back to the cemetery. Neither of us said much on the way. A self-consciousness seemed to come over us, as if the misty light of day had dissipated the magic of the previous hour. We rode back as we had ridden in, not in the embarrassed silence of two strangers suddenly thrown together who know nothing of each other, but in the embarrassed silence of two strangers who have revealed too much of themselves.

The rain stopped and within minutes Bryan had the tire changed.

"Well, I guess that does it," he said, cleaning his hands with a rag he took out of the trunk.

He looked as if he wanted to say more, but I spoke up.

"Thanks so much," I said, avoiding his eyes. "I mean it, you really were a lifesaver." I dug into my pocket. "If I can pay—"

"Would you want to try again sometime?" he blurted. "Take Sam up on his offer, I mean?"

I hesitated. I couldn't hide my troubled expression. "I did enjoy myself, honestly. It was... different, so unexpected, but... I really don't know anything about you and—"

"*Now* who's being cynical?" he said, forcing a smile and throwing the words out like a challenge.

I met his smile with a wry one of my own. "All right, you've made your point."

"Good," he said, trying not to sound too enthusiastic. "If you give me your phone number ..." he searched for his pen "...and the best time to call is...."

"Weekdays I'm usually home by nine. Weekends are more chancey..."

* * * * *

I saw him in my rear view mirror, standing there watching me, his hand raised, as I drove the winding lane out of the cemetery. It all seemed too crazy and mysterious to be true.

Chapter 3

Sitting cross-legged on her bed, Lisa looked up from her movie magazine when I barged into our apartment, kicked off my shoes, flung my jacket over a chair and bolted for the bathroom.

Lisa called peevishly over the music blaring from her radio, "Well! Hello to you, too, Carly."

She went on ranting until I came out of the bathroom with my mirror and humming *You Made Me Love You,* the last song Sam played for us. "Hi Lisa," I said, plopping myself on the edge of my bed and combing the tangles out of my hair.

"Hi yourself," she snapped, tossing her magazine aside and poking her designer glasses into place with a stubby finger. "I expected you back a lot sooner. The least you could do is call me if you're going to be late." Lisa tugged at her faded pink robe and patted the red curlers anchored to her damp head. "Carly, I'm *talking* to you." She stretched across the bed to the radio and lowered the volume. "I said you could have called. What happened to three o'clock?"

"I'm sorry, Lisa, I guess I wasn't thinking."

Lisa plucked the big clippers from her manicure kit on the bed stand. "You weren't thinking, but I was. All sorts of terrible things."

Grunting, she cranked her foot into a cutting position and wrapped her arms around her leg. "Someday when I'm rich, I swear it, I'm going to have a slave to do this job for me," she grumbled. "Or any guy who wants to marry me is going to have to promise to give me a pedicure every week."

Cheek to knee, she snipped her red toenails until the roll of

28

flab across her midsection cut off her wind, forcing her to rest against her padded headboard. "Yes, as proof of his love, my personal slave." Slowly she raised her leg. "But first, Jacque," she said, pointing her toes, "kiss them. Tenderly, one by one."

Lisa's terry-cloth robe fell apart, exposing her legs. "But not until *you* do something about these," she chided herself, slapping her chunky thighs and pulling herself together.

"You'll never guess where I was," I said, interrupting the fantasy I'd heard her recite so many times before I could give it back verbatim.

"I'm not in the mood for guessing games right now, Carly," she said sarcastically.

"In a cemetery," I said, primping in my mirror.

Lisa's jaw dropped. "In a what?"

"A cemetery. Forest Lawn."

"What in the world were—What happened, Carly?"

"Just a little ol' flat tire."

Lisa's round, green eyes opened wide. "You got a flat tire in the cemetery?"

I studied my face at an angle in the mirror. "Smack in the middle of it."

Lisa shuddered. "My God, that's terrible, Carly. What did you do?"

"What could I do? I hitched a ride out in a funeral hearse." I threw myself back on my bed, laughing.

"Ha ha, Carly, very funny, very funny. Here I am, worried to death something happened to you, imagining all kinds of crazy things like you got mugged or raped or something, and you tell me you almost got trapped in a cemetery and now you sit around making jokes."

"I didn't know you cared," I teased, dropping the mirror, twisting around and stretching out on my side.

Lisa lifted her puggy nose in the air. "Don't flatter yourself, Carly. It's only that I need somebody to help pay the rent on this penthouse."

"Penthouses aren't on the first floor, Lisa, and they're much more expensive."

"So? Feel rich. Don't look out the window." She tucked her leg up and resumed clipping her toenails.

I plumped up my pillow and rolled onto my back.

Lisa frowned. "What were you doing in a cemetery, anyway?"

Carly gazed into her mirror, "Lisa, do you think my eyes are set too close?"

Lisa sat back. "Set too close to what?"

I tilted the mirror. "Someone told me once that I look oriental."

"As far as I know, Chinese don't have blue eyes. Black hair, like you, maybe, I guess, but not blue eyes."

"I mean because they are a little slanted." I ran my finger under my eye.

"Look, Madame Wu, if you're fishing for compliments, you've come to the wrong place. Which reminds me, I made some chow mein. It's on the counter, but you'll have to warm it up if you want some. I had mine already."

"So early?"

"I shouldn't have had it at all. It gives me gas, and there's nothing worse than suffering with gas when you're on a date."

"Maybe I'll do something different," I said, thinking aloud.

"Why? It's tasty. You liked it last time."

"My hair, I mean." I plucked at my temples. "A page boy, but no, that's so out of date. A wedge cut? Maybe a pixie. Is that too old-fashioned, too?"

"Whatever. I don't think they're for you. For me they're fine. My face is round, too round to suit me, but yours is more... oval."

"Long hair is such a bother." I smoothed back the side. "The Sassoon look, then, or have I been watching too many old movies? I haven't really been keeping up. I hate all these stringy styles that make you look like a Raggedy Ann mop head that just crawled out of bed. And I don't like the braided look that takes half a day to do, either, not to mention the cost."

Lisa set her clippers aside and picked up the nail file. "All right, Carly," she said, narrowing her eyes, "what's going on?"

"Why, Lisa, whatever *do* you mean?"

"Don't play mind-games with me, Carly. You don't live and work with somebody as long as I have without getting to know them pretty good. Since when did you ever worry about how your hair looks?" She mimicked me: "Would it look better this way or that? Long or short? Black or blonde?"

"Blonde. You know, Lisa, I was a blonde a few years before we met. I'm really bored with this look. Maybe I'll go back to blonde again."

"Your eyes, too? You're not happy with them anymore, either? Uh uh, Carly. You've been acting weird ever since you waltzed through that door, and you know it. So will you quit avoiding the issue? And *kindly* take your face out of that mirror

31

and tell me what happened today?"

"Nothing, really. I had a flat tire and somebody helped me fix it, that's all."

"Somebody? What somebody? A guy?"

"Yes, a guy."

"You could have called me."

"I would have, but I didn't have my phone and his battery was dead." I giggled. "Get it, Lisa? In the cemetery, the battery was dead?"

"Ha ha. You slay me, Carly. Get it? Slay me…hmmm?"

"Ouch."

"Don't try to get off the subject, Carly. How does it take two or three hours to fix a flat tire?"

"We had to wait. The garage was busy."

"We? And why a garage?"

"The spare tire was flat in the trunk, so we had to take it to a garage and have it fixed. See?"

Lisa nodded slowly, frowning, like she was trying to absorb the facts. "You and this guy. Together. Uh-huh. I could tell the minute you came in, Carly, the way you floated out of the bathroom over to your bed, all dreamy-like— I knew something fishy was going on."

"Fishy? Actually, they were salty little ones."

Lisa knitted her pale eyebrows. "Huh?"

"In the antipasto."

"Carly, this guy didn't slip you something, did he? You know, one of those date- rape drugs that guys have been using. You're not flipping out on me, are you?"

"But they really do nothing for the breath?"

"What *are* you talking about?"

"Anchovies, silly."

"Carly, will you put that damn mirror down and talk sense… Caar—ly!"

I laid aside the mirror, stretched out and rolled onto my side again. "There really is nothing mysterious about it," I said, propping my head on my hand. "He was nice enough to help me out when he saw I was stranded there in the cemetery, that's all."

"Well, what did you do all that time?"

"He taught me how to start the car if I have carburetor trouble." I burst out laughing, remembering the shock and then the embarrassment on his face when I told him the problem was a flat tire, like a show-off kid riding no hands on his bike and running smack into a tree.

"What's so funny? Wait, don't tell me. I had to be there, right?"

"Right."

"Come on, Carly, out with it, what happened?"

"We had coffee and a salad in a nice little Italian restaurant next door to the garage while we were waiting to get the tire fixed." I raked my hair with my free hand. "Nothing really special."

"Oh, no, nothing special, sure, not much. Well, what's he like? What did he say? Is he good looking? Are you going to see him again? Could you tell if he's rich?"

"He's just an average guy."

Lisa scoffed. "Yeah, sure, just an average guy."

"Well, maybe a cut above." I twirled a strand of hair around my finger, thinking. "Brownish hair, wavy and not rock-hard and pasted down with styling gel."

"How could you tell?"

"Otherwise the wind couldn't blow it around the way it did."

"Anything else you noticed about this so-called average guy who just conveniently happened to be hanging around in a cemetery?"

"He did have a nice nose," I said wistfully. "Curved up a little. And very kissable lips."

"Carly, you didn't let him kiss you!"

"Of course not...and hazel eyes." I broke up laughing again, remembering the trunk lid hitting his head. "Make that *watery*, hazel eyes."

"Carly, are you cracking up, or what? What did you have to drink— and don't tell me just coffee."

"Well, we did share some wine."

"Oh, my God. Smart, very smart. You just meet some guy, a perfect stranger on the other side of the city, and the two of you spend the afternoon together sucking up wine."

"Harry James was there, too."

"Harry James. Who's he?"

"A trumpet player."

"A what?"

"Actually, a dead trumpet player."

"Carly, you are exasperating. I ask a simple question and nothing but crazy answers come out of your mouth. What are you trying to hide?"

"Not a thing, Lisa. You're just looking for more than is there."

"Oh, am I?" she said, looking askance. "Well take a good look at yourself, all of yourself, stretching and squirming so sensually all over the bed like a lovesick cat." She began picking the nail clippings from her lavender quilt and collected them in the cup of her hand. "So are you at least going to tell me his name?"

"Bryan. I think he said his last name is Perri. Yes, that's it, Bryan Perri."

"Two first names?" Lisa cocked her head. "He doesn't sound rich. Is he big, small or what?"

"Oh, around six feet I'd guess. Trim, too, as far as I could tell, with his suit coat on. Very respectable looking."

"Oh, sure. So was Ted Bundy. Don't you remember that TV program we saw about serial killers. He was one of them. But if you're going to take a chance, I guess it's better than if he's dressed like a bum. Did you make a date with him?"

"No, but I think he'll call to ask for one."

Lisa rolled her eyes. "She thinks! Well, I know he will."

"I'm not sure I'll accept."

Lisa looked at me sharply. "The creeps at the restaurant who hit on you, sure, you'll turn them down. This one, though— what's his name, Bryan? ...I think you won't. Not that it'll do him any good. The minute he starts getting serious, he'll be finished. Like all the others."

"Lisa, you make me sound like a monster. You know very well I'm not interested in a permanent relationship."

"Not interested in a per-ma-nent re-lation-ship," Lisa mimicked. "I wish you'd stop with those dumb college expressions, Carly, and say you don't want to go steady. You're just afraid to fall in love. You know it and I know it. I only wish I knew why."

I started to get angry, but checked myself. "Maybe you're right, Lisa. Why bother in the first place if I don't want to get serious with someone."

Lisa stammered. "I'm sorry, Carly, I shouldn't have said that. It's really none of my business."

"Don't feel bad, Lisa. You're just reading too much into everything."

"It's so hard to understand you, Carly. We've been roommates for more than two years and I can't say I know you, the real Carly. You're beautiful, twenty-five years old, or is it twenty-six? You're smart and getting smarter all the time with school and all, and yet you avoid getting serious with anyone like the plague. Honestly, you baffle me."

"Relationships are trouble, Lisa. Did you ever see one that wasn't? It's either money or jealousy or drugs or politics or—"

"Yes, Carly, I know. It's called life. But it doesn't have to be all those things. It depends on who you pick and what you make of it. Anyway, if you won't think of yourself, think of me. After you drop them, who answers the phone calls asking what they did wrong or say wrong, or is there somebody else, and can I fix it up somehow. I feel like I'm your mother or a miracle worker. And sometimes I get cursed out, too, like it's my fault you don't want to have anything to do with them."

"You're exaggerating, Lisa. I have my job and I have school. I don't need the extra pressure... which reminds me...." I reached under my bed and dragged out a stack of books.

Lisa scowled. "Remember those two guys, Joe and Bob we double-dated a couple of times last year? He was really nice, that Joe, but no, you had to kill it because he was getting too serious. And that made Bob quit me. Good-looking guys, too, real hunks, both of them. I'd give anything to have guys eating out of my hand like you do. I wouldn't care how serious they got. If you want to know the real truth, I'd love it."

I thumbed through a book. "It's kinder to end it soon, before it goes too far because then you can't be accused of leading them on. It's dangerous. There are too many nuts out there who become obsessed and can't take rejection. Lisa," I said, growing weary with arguing, "is there anything wrong with just wanting to be friends, to go to a movie with or to dinner?"

"You mean purely a platonic relationship."

"Yes. Exactly. Someone to spend time with discussing the great issues of life, without getting seriously involved."

"No, of course there's nothing wrong with it, but—"

"Well, you make it sound like there is. I don't happen to like the hassle that goes with the territory. And I don't like being looked upon like a freak because I refuse to go to bed with them, or see their eyes open like saucers when I tell them I'm not that type and don't intend to start now. So they get ticked and our little relationship ends.

"There aren't many virgins left these days, Carly. I'm sure those guys don't believe you anyway."

"Who cares what they think. All I know is I don't have to answer to anyone about what I do with my body or why. I won't have any guilt and therefore no regrets. My life is my own, completely my own— no explanations and no obligations to anybody but myself. I'm not giving anybody power over me, because that's exactly what happens when a girl is easy and gives in. From that moment on she becomes vulnerable. Now the guy's got her where he wants her, gets possessive and she loses control over her life, and maybe her self-respect, too. It's a well worn pattern, Lisa, but not for me, thank you."

Lisa plugged in her hair dryer. "You know, Carly, you're smart, much smarter than me when it comes to books, but when it comes to real life, you're just plain dumb. Excuse me, but that's the word, dumb! And I'm not jealous, if that's what you're thinking. Or maybe I am in a way, I don't know. But you're my friend, Carly. Even more than that; you're like my older sister, and I wish you'd stop kidding yourself. I think you're afraid of getting hurt, but you have to face reality sometime and stop making excuses for dumping every guy you meet. You can't keep running from life and hiding behind your fancy words and ideas forever. Sure, what you say all sounds good and even makes sense, in a way, especially in today's world. Just the same, I think you're asking for trouble. You act like every guy out there wants to punish you somehow or take advantage of you. Maybe some guy hurt you or ditched you in the past, I don't know, but I don't believe they're all that way. With that attitude of yours, though, Carly, sooner or later you're going to learn what it really means to get hurt. Or end up a lonely old lady in a rocking chair looking out the window and wishing you'd have done things differently, wondering what it would have been like to have children and grandchildren helping you bake cookies or trimming the Christmas tree, seeing them grow up and having them to confide in and be there for you when you need them. The trouble with you, Carly, is that you think too much. Or maybe not enough."

I closed my book and set it aside. "Now that you've brought it up, look who's asking for trouble. Don't take this wrong, Lisa, and I'm not saying it to be vindictive or because I want to hurt you, but do you think it's wise going out tonight with this... this Dave?"

Lisa bristled. "David. And you're right, it is none of your business."

"Lisa, I'm only bringing it up because he's so much older than you. And you don't know a thing about him except that he likes his eggs over light and his bacon crisp."

Lisa flounced around, dropping a few curlers on the floor. "I know more about him than you know about this Bryan. David's been coming into the restaurant for...for quite a while now. He's friendly, never complains and... and he's not too old for me. I'm twenty—"

"Nineteen."

"Almost twenty, and pretty mature, if I do say so myself. If I don't know my mind well enough to pick my dates by now I never will." Her lips quivered in her round face. "I'm sick of immature boys, if you must know. They're crude and cheap and stuck on themselves. They always end up hurting you."

"Lisa, what's the matter with the guy who smothers his eggs in ketchup? The one from the school. He seems to like you and always sits in your section. He's always smiling and pleasant. He never complains. Isn't it worth giving him a chance?"

"Him? The one who's always telling me I should read some book or other and talks like he's got marbles in his mouth? Give me a break, Carly, I'm not that desperate yet."

"Well, how about the one who always sits in the corner booth, the one with the loud, knitted sweaters? He seems to have eyes for you."

"That creep? Always writing in his notebook and eating French fries? What a wimp. What is he, sixteen? Give me credit for something better than that."

"Oh, Lisa, how can you say those things? The bookworm is friendly and interesting. So he mumbles when he talks; at least he's interesting and talks sense. And the sweater guy seems sweet. I waited on him, too, I know. He's older than sixteen and nice looking. He always sits in your section. You know he's interested. He's just shy; you can tell by the way he won't look you straight in the eye and how flushed he gets when he orders from you. You told me so yourself. You don't even give him a chance to talk to you, and you can see he'd like to. You don't really have any idea what he's like."

"And I'm not interested in finding out," she sneered. "With his 1960s Beatles haircut and sad eyes, like he's seeing a car wreck. Besides, he's probably like all the rest, maybe only a good actor who hasn't shown his true colors yet."

"You're taking a lot for granted, Lisa. He has a nice smile, you have to admit. And he's not a wise guy or a jerk. Why don't you at least give him a chance? Or give the bookworm a chance. In other words, date someone, anyone, more your own age. If you're going to take a risk dating, date someone you're more likely to have something in common with."

"*You* give him a chance. Go date him. He's all yours. And marble-mouth bookworm, too." She threw out her hands. "I give them both to you. And there's that other one, too, don't forget him, the lean bean with the liver lips, always staring at me. I've been out with others, too. Take them all, Carly."

"It's you they're interested in, Lisa. It's you they like, obviously."

"Too bad. I want somebody I know is mature, somebody who's not out to use me or try to make a fool out of me or try to get me into bed after the first kiss. I want to be treated with respect, Carly, the same way I treat them."

I couldn't hold back a weary sigh. "Lisa, where does this David live? What does he do for a living? Are you even sure he's single?"

Lisa flushed a pink to match her housecoat. "Oh, that was a low blow, Carly, a cheap shot, trying to make me suspicious. What am I supposed to do, interview him first? Get references? His social security number? 'Fill out this application, sir. Sign here, sir. I'll get in touch if I can use you, sir.'"

"Lisa, Lisa, I don't mean to hurt you. You're right, we are like sisters. But you're the one who mentioned facing reality. Well, ask yourself, where can this lead? I'll bet he's at least a dozen years older than you. So many others are out there, more your age, more suitable."

"Oh, really? Well, where the heck are they? I mean the decent ones, not the punks or the losers you mentioned. You don't hear the phone ringing off the hook, do you? I'm not beautiful like you, Carly. You got them drooling in their cups and falling off the counter stools, and you don't give them a tumble. You always get the pick of the crop." Her eyes misted over. "You eat more than I do and never gain an ounce. I'm fat and ugly. I'm not kidding myself, Carly. You got it all. I can't afford to be so particular like you can."

"Lisa, oh Lisa, why do you put yourself down all the time? You're not fat and you're not ugly."

"Well, you can't deny it, can you, whenever a couple of guys are near us, who do they throw themselves at? I might as well be invisible. I lied to myself for a long time, thinking I'm not so bad to look at and it's the kind of person you are inside that really counts, your personality, and who you are in your heart that really matters. Well, I was wrong, and all the junk they write about in books about your 'inner beauty' is a pack of rotten lies. I know what I am now, and it's not what guys want. Not for life, anyway. As soon as I slap their hands off my breast and fight with them a few minutes, they're done with me." She dug a tissue from her pocket.

I rose and sat down beside her on the bed and slid my arm around her shoulder.

"Don't, Carly, don't give me any sympathy, please, or I'll really break down."

"You're so wrong, Lisa. I wish I could make you believe me. You're sweet and lovable and pretty." I squeezed her arm. "Yes, pretty. I just wish you wouldn't be so hard on yourself and anxious, Lisa. The right guy will come along in time, someone more suitable, someone deserving of you. Be patient. You don't have to grab on to just anybody. An older man isn't necessarily mature, you know. He can be even more devious than someone young, if for no other reason than that he's had more experience."

Lisa shrugged against my comforting arm. "Sometimes I hate you, Carly, just hate you. It's easy for you to say those things." Lisa's face tightened. "Do you remember when I came home early from a date with that young jerk... the creep with the black, wavy hair you thought was so nice?"

"The blind date Sara set you up with a couple of months ago?"

"Yes, him. Remember how pleasant and friendly he was, making his little jokes?" She pulled away and looked into my eyes. "I couldn't tell you before because I was ashamed... so ashamed."

"Of what, Lisa, ashamed of what?"

"Remember the first time he picked me up here? I should've known by the look on his face when he laid eyes on me that he thought I was a huge disappointment, but I didn't want to believe it. Not that he was the greatest looking guy himself I'd ever seen, if you want to know the truth."

"Well, then...?"

"We drove to the Studio 6 show and everything seemed all right. We talked a lot on the way over. He even seemed kind of warm, kind of…." She choked up.

"He got fresh? Is that what you're trying to say, he tried to take advantage of you? Lisa, you know it's par for the course these days. And it's not only young guys who do it. A lot of older ones are impatient, too. We've all lived through the same rotten experience and it's exactly what I don't want to be involved in."

"I wish he had tried to get fresh. That I could understand. It would at least mean I'm attractive or desirable."

"Lisa!"

"No, Carly, it was even worse, a lot worse. He pulled up in front of the show and let me out so I wouldn't have to walk from the parking lot. I told him it was okay, that I didn't mind walking, but he insisted. 'A gentleman doesn't let a lady walk if he can help it,' he said, so I got out of the car and waited for him." Tears streamed from her eyes. "And I waited, Carly. And I waited, standing on the sidewalk, stretching my neck, looking, five minutes, ten minutes, then I thought something must have happened to him. I worried that he got mugged or fell down in the lot and broke something. I went searching, up one row and down the other, but he wasn't there, his car wasn't there. He was gone. At first I couldn't believe it. Then the truth hit me in the face. I was shocked to think anyone could be so cruel to another person. I felt like a fool. A horrible fool.

"I couldn't hide from the truth anymore, Carly. He dumped me, dumped me like a stinking bag of garbage." She sobbed into her hands. "I didn't deserve it. Why did he do it to me, Carly, why? Am I so fat and ugly he couldn't stand to be with me or be seen with me, even for a couple of hours? Whores don't get treated like that! I walked the streets for hours. I cried and cried. I wanted to die. I was so humiliated I wanted to throw myself in front of a car and kill myself." She fell into my arms, choking with pain. "Oh, Carly, why am I here? What good am I to anyone? I hate my life, I hate myself. I wish I could die."

I held her close, saying nothing. We stayed like that a long time, Lisa's shoulders convulsing with sobs coming from some deep place within her. At last she pulled away, wiping her eyes with her sleeve and sinking back on her bed.

"No guy ever dumped you and left you cold, Carly. You never had to sit home alone watching TV while your friends were all out on a date or at a party you weren't invited to. You were never humiliated when the guys picked partners for double dates and you were ignored. Well, maybe now you can understand why I'm going to see David. He's mature. He's decent to me, he gives me attention. He makes me feel like a woman. He makes me feel *wanted.* Do you understand what I mean, Carly, to actually feel like I'm worthwhile and wanted? If you want the truth I've already been out with him, more than a couple of times. A lot more."

Her words surprised me. "Lisa, you never said anything about it to me."

"He didn't want me to. He said it was nobody's business but our own. And what we did and where we went was private."

"Lisa...Lisa, you didn't....you haven't..."

"Let's drop the subject, all right, Carly? Please? No more questions." She straightened up, smoothing her face. "Oh, God, what must I look like!" She bounded up and snatched the mirror off my bed. "Look at me, Carly, just look at me. A total mess and he'll be here in less than an hour."

"Okay, Lisa," I said, rising, "do what you think is best. I still don't think you're making the right decision, but who really knows? Anyway, it's your life, after all."

I crossed to the kitchen area, slipped my plate of chow mein into the microwave oven and punched in the time. I felt oddly guilty, as if I were somehow responsible for Lisa's unhappiness. Of course I couldn't understand the depth of her misery. I'd never had a problem getting boyfriends; in fact, it was just the opposite with me. How ironic, Lisa desperately wanted a serious relationship and I did everything possible to avoid one. Life plays funny tricks on people. A bitterness rose in my throat remembering what Lisa had said about her not knowing what it was like to have a guy leave her cold. Well, Lisa didn't know everything!

I took the plate from the oven, suddenly realizing I wasn't the least bit hungry and set it aside.

Lisa padded barefoot into the kitchen. "I'm sorry, Carly. I shouldn't unload my troubles on you. It isn't fair. I wish I could be more like you. You seem able to handle things so much better than I do."

"Don't be so hard on yourself, Lisa. And don't kid yourself, I'm not as perfect and my life isn't as rosy as you seem to think." I remembered Bryan's words about people not being all they appeared to be. "I'm just not very comfortable talking about myself." I leaned against the counter and folded my arms. "Maybe when we get a little time we can have a nice heart to heart talk with no personal attacks or accusations or anything hurtful. I really would like to know what you actually want out of life, what's most important to you."

"That's easy," Lisa said, pulling out her curlers, "A man, that's what I want. I'm not getting any younger."

"Lisa, you're not even out of your teens."

"You know how time flies. Before you know it, you're an old maid. No, Carly, I want marriage, security. Simple as that, Carly. Kids and a home of my own."

"You forgot love, Lisa."

Lisa flushed. "Of course—love. That goes without saying. I was going to say love."

The phone rang and Lisa fairly pounced on it. "Hello... No, this is her roommate. Who's calling, please...? Yes, she is," she answered dryly, "hold on." She held the phone up. "You *think* he'll call."

I waved bye-bye to Lisa and took the phone:

"Yes...? Yes, I got home safe... Oh, my roommate, Lisa. We work together, too. Very sweet, yes, she is...." I laughed softly. "No, no carburetor trouble, either...."

We spoke a few minutes, then:

"Sorry, I really can't tonight. I have some reading for class and tomorrow comes early... Tomorrow night I have school... Wednesday, too... No, I'm not putting you off... All right, then, Friday... seven's fine...."

I gave Bryan my address and said goodbye three different times before he finally let me go. I stood a moment beside the phone, feeling an odd sense of excitement I hadn't known before. Or did I just forget? Sometimes it's hard to remember the past, especially when you spend so much time trying to forget it. The sound of Bryan's voice, warm and intimate, still lingered in my memory. The way— How foolish I am! Lisa's right, I barely know him. I should have broken it off right then and there, ended it before—

"Well, that was short and sweet," Lisa said, coming back into the room, brushing her hair. "What is he, a car mechanic?"

I flopped down on my bed. "Eavesdropping, Lisa?"

"He didn't waste any time calling, did he?"

"He only wanted to make sure I got home safely."

"Uh huh. So when are you going out with him?"

"You mean you didn't hear? Not that it matters. I'll see him Friday." I opened my book. "It will probably be for the last time."

"Fat chance of that, if he has anything to say about it… And what's with wicked smile I see on your face?"

"I have an idea. It might show me what he's really like. A kind of test of his mettle, his character."

Lisa paused and put her hair brush down. "You know, Carly, you should print up rejection slips and hand them out to the poor slobs. It would be so much easier on you."

"No, Lisa, this time I think it will be the other way around. I'm sure he'll realize I'm not his type."

"Oh, sure, like bees don't like flowers anymore."

"Now if you'll kindly let me catch up on my reading…."

I flicked the pages and tried to read but my mind wouldn't allow me to concentrate on the words. My thoughts drifted back to the afternoon, to the moment I first saw him approaching with that silly grin on his face. Even then, despite my fear of meeting a stranger in such a place, I felt a tremor, a thrill, a subdued sense of excitement. A fluttering sense of danger and relief all at once. Whatever it was, I saw him again as I did then, tall and handsome, a little wind-blown, magically appearing out of nowhere like a knight in shining armor.

Handsome, yes, but not *that* handsome. Certainly no Adonis. If the truth be known, I had rebuffed quite a number of guys who were better looking. A few even far better looking.

So why couldn't I get him out of my mind? Ordinarily, men who threw themselves at me turned me off instantly. They always gave me the impression of being spineless. I couldn't

47

respect them. But didn't Bryan show himself that way, too? How could I deny that he was almost literally falling-down anxious to please me? He annoyed me, too. Yet, in some peculiar, unexplainable way, he had charmed me. More than charmed me. Why why why?

Was there something about myself I didn't understand and had to learn before I could be hurt, a chink in the formidable armor of my defenses he could sense? And that glimmer of a smile on his face when I spoke, as if he could see behind my words, see past me to an inner self I was hiding or wasn't aware of, that mocking expression in those mesmerizing hazel-green eyes that made me feel like the canary in the famous fable. Nor could I escape the feeling that, although he seemed to be throwing himself at me, he was in fact manipulating me. If so, I had to be careful, very careful. So far I had won against a wide range of approaches, but the odds dictated the coming of a nemesis. I had once heard that everyone has a nemesis in life.

The words blurred on the page and I lowered the book to my breast.

In his own way, though, Bryan was different. Unlike most men I'd met, he didn't seem afraid to appear weak in a woman's eyes. Hadn't he faced up to his embarrassment in the cemetery with a smile, albeit a rather wan one? That in itself said something of his self-esteem, his self-confidence. He struck me as solid, real, as someone genuinely interested in me as a person, unlike those others whose lustful eyes saw me as a prize, as something to bed down, who boasted and spoke of nothing all evening but themselves.

Still, I had to be on guard and not be lulled by his charm. He might be only more clever than the others. After all, didn't he himself say the truth is not on the surface? Of course I disagreed with him on that, but didn't people often judge others by themselves? Wasn't there an old sarcastic response about having to 'be one to know one'? He could be the most devious of all. And why wasn't he married? Or did he hide his wedding band in his pocket? Men can be sneaky if they want something badly enough.

So many questions; so much to think about. Lisa said I'd find trouble, that I'd be hurt. I prayed not. Not if I could possibly help it. No, I couldn't bear it, not again.

I closed my eyes and dozed off.

I dreamed:

...a face, mottled among the tombstones, peering at me as I sat in a wing chair sipping wine. Strangers, formally dressed, mill around, blocking my view. Some are dancing a waltz. I rise, surprised to see myself dressed in a white party gown. A trumpet is playing 'Cherry,' but I can't locate its source. My mother and father glide past. I'm pleased to see them well and smiling happily as I begin to twirl like a ballerina. My dress flares and I'm amazed that my wine glass, held high, doesn't spill.

Through the crowd I see a stranger stealing the tires from my car. I want to cry out, but I'm fascinated by the easy flow of his body as he moves from one side to the other. Someone taps my shoulder. I spin around and find myself looking into a pair of intense blue eyes. Embarrassed, I draw back. I know this man, but can't remember his name. He smiles and reaches into his pocket. He is going to surprise me with a gift, I'm certain.

Suddenly he whips out a breadstick and waves it in my face, slowly, back and forth. Horrified, I spill my wine. An ugly red stain spreads over my breast, down my gown. I scream and begin to run. Behind me, someone is laughing. I stumble and fall. My shoes are gone and my stockings are torn. I'm frantic and begin to cry. My arms are scraped, my hands bloody. I pick myself up and run again.

I reach a high iron fence, black, with tips like spears. A cemetery! I'm terrified. Outside, on the other side, almost beyond view, Lisa is calling: "Carly, I'm leaving now!" I try to call out, to tell her not to go, to help me, but my voice is gone. I can't breathe—

I woke with a start, wet with perspiration. Over the music playing softly on the radio I heard the click of the door closing behind Lisa as she left for her date with David.

Chapter 4

I lathered my face thinking how much I hate shaving. How much of my life am I going to spend on this chore? Let me see: ten minutes each day, say, six days a week, fifty-two weeks a year. That would come to an hour a week times fifty-two, which would be fifty-two hours a year. And that would be the equivalent of six and a half working days. More than a full work week a year!

I was careful not to nick myself again as I gingerly drew the blade along my jaw, swished my razor in the bowl and rode up against the grain under my chin.

Let's assume I live to seventy-five," I said aloud to better hold the figures in my mind, "minus, say, the first seventeen years, which comes to... fifty-eight years." Carefully, I scraped the space between my nose and upper lip.

Let's see now...fifty-two times fifty-eight equals....heck. Let's round it off to fifty times fifty, which would be...twenty-five hundred hours. And I could probably add a few hundred more to that." I tried to whistle my amazement, but the soap encroaching on my lips smothered the sound.

After a little more calculating, I realized I'll be spending about a year standing before a mirror performing a job on a face that's not going to get any better looking. Even if I can cut the time in half, I'm still looking at six solid months of my life! I decided to practice shaving more quickly. Cutting off even a minute each time would add up to weeks in the long run.

I ran the blade a final time over my chin. Shaving once in the morning was bad enough, but doing it again in the evening on special occasions like this was pure torture. Tonight was worth it though; I wanted to look my very best. Light as my beard is, I didn't want to take a chance on looking grungy.

Finished, I rinsed my face and gave it a close inspection in the mirror. Miracle of miracles, no nicks! I considered it a small victory over myself. And a good omen, too, I thought, splashing on some Old Spice lotion.

Now, what to wear? If only Carly had given me some idea of where she'd like to go... I fingered through my tie rack, wondering why she cut me short on the phone. She accepted the date only after I pressed her. She might see it as repayment of a debt. No, that didn't seem to be it. Despite her words, the peculiar tone of her voice carried a different message. Maybe Carly didn't want to talk in front of what's-her-name... Liza or Lisa, with the chill in her voice, the one I called sweet, hoping that word would be conveyed in case I need a future ally....

I picked a gold tie to go with a pair of tan slacks and white shirt. The tie I could slip off, if necessary, and my brown leather jacket would fit almost any occasion. I put myself together, slapped on an extra dose of shaving lotion and headed out the door.

Cruising at a steady clip in light traffic, I made good time across town. I knew her area, not well, but well enough not to get lost. It was an older Polish neighborhood, clean but beginning to wear down, not far from the university and the restaurant where she worked.

As I drove along, my mind went back to Sam's restaurant, to the moment my name dropped from Carly's lips for the first time, those gorgeous, moist, full lips shaping themselves around my name: *Bryan...* my name on her sweet and precious breath, rolling like honey off her tongue: *Bryan...* my name now etched in her mind, forever a part of her, joining me to her existence: *Bryan.. .*my name sounded with music in it, familiarity, a hint of intimacy, my spoken name tearing down the barrier of anonymity between us and forming a bridge to her heart.

She surprised me when she said she was a waitress. I would've guessed she was a social worker or a teacher, but, yes, I could visualize her as a waitress now: reserved, poised, wearing a white or chartreuse headband setting off her flowing black hair... beautiful, alert, efficient, the kind of girl who could charm the grouchiest of customers or freeze some jerk with those chilling-blue eyes.

Then there was the brief time when we listened to the words to *You Made Me Love You.* In the flickering candlelight, like shadows of passing clouds over a landscape, I saw her changing moods, now remote, now melancholic, now mysterious, now dangerous.

Gradually, we came 'round to each other again. Our eyes met, rather self-consciously, I thought. She smiled and a whole universe of emotion erupted in me, a confused, exhilarating and dismaying universe that opened a new world of feelings I didn't know existed.

I remembered again my last moments with her in the cemetery, waving until I could no longer see her as she wound her way down the winding path to the street. I gazed across to the gravestones, jutting like gray, stone teeth in the jaws of a dying day. I wondered, could love be born in such a forbidding place?

I turned into her street and followed the house numbers down until I spotted her apartment. It was one of several in a converted family home standing near the corner of the street squeezed with narrow two-family houses, their porches half-hidden by ancient shrubbery footing miniature lawns.

A few minutes early, I circled the block a couple of times trying to calm the butterflies playing tag in my stomach, and rehearsing the lines I might use. When she opens the door I'll step back, look slightly astonished and say:

"Hi, Carly, you look absolutely lovely."

No, 'lovely' sounded too wimpy.

"Hi, Carly, you look great."

No good, either. Too empty. Too trite.

"Hi, Carly, you look terrific."

Same thing.

"Hi, Carly, you look beautiful."

Too much too soon.

"Hi, Carly, you look fabulous."

Overkill.

Forget it! I drew in a deep breath to ease the tension. Be nonchalant, I reminded myself. Try too hard and you'll tighten up and blow the whole thing. What's the big deal anyway, I thought. She's just another girl she's just another girl she's just...

I wheeled up to an open space two doors down, adjusted my tie and climbed out. Her car, parked behind mine, didn't appear quite as shabby in the dull light. But it still looked a little sad and pathetic, the same way Carly looked the first time I saw her standing beside it.

I gave the tires the once-over as I passed, and when I looked up I was surprised to see her coming down the walk.

I stopped. "Hi, Carly, ...jeez...you, uh, you—"

"Hi," she said, closing the gap between us. "Any trouble finding my place?" Her pony tail, bobbing with her steps, lent a frisky aspect to the sedate and proper girl I remembered from a few days earlier.

"None at all," I said, turning up the sidewalk with her. "I've had business not far from here."

"I'm glad. Some people find the streets around here confusing." She flashed a smile that tingled my blood. "Your car or mine?"

"Mine's warmed up," I said, touching the arm of her fringed, white leather jacket. She was wearing a brown-and-white checked skirt that ended just above her knees. Maybe she had a rodeo in mind. All she needed was a cowboy hat, I thought, and we could have taken horses.

Before I could get the handle, she had her hand on it. "I'll get it," she said, opening the door and helping herself in.

I circled the car, not quite knowing what to make of her behavior. Was it a show of independence? And why the impish smile and that gleam in her eye?

"I, uh, like your jacket," I said, settling in next to her and fishing for my key. "Very striking."

"Oh, thanks. I didn't really know what to wear.... Did you have anyplace special in mind?"

"Nothing particular, but I hear the play at the Little Theater's pretty good. We can get tickets at the door if you're interested. Or a movie if you like or—"

"What's the play?"

"I believe it's a Tennessee Williams'—"

"Oh, he's too depressing for my taste." She wrinkled her nose. "I don't think so."

I fired up the engine. "Any suggestions?" I asked, glancing away to hide my disappointment. I didn't think she'd turn down a good play, being a college girl and no doubt intellectually inclined.

"As a matter of fact—" She dug into her tiny clutch bag and brought out a slip. "How do you feel about pool?"

"Pool?" Now *that* I never expected, especially from her. "You mean like with a stick and billiard balls?"

"I don't mean with a butterfly or backstroke."

Again I saw that mischievous glint in her eyes. Amused, I smiled. "Can you play?"

"Of course I can," she shot back, hinting mock indignation. "I play at the student lounge sometimes when I have time and… and other places."

She amused me, this twenty-something year old acting like a self-indulgent teenager who'd rather play pool than see a famous play or even a decent movie. Maybe she just needed a temporary diversion. "Okay," I said, pulling away from the curb, "if that's what you want. The Metro Billiard Parlor on State Street shouldn't be too crowded yet, but you never know."

She held the slip up to catch the light. "No, not there. I think I'd like to try… Willy's Pool Palace."

She caught me by surprise. "Willy's Pool Palace? Where's that?"

"On… Blake Street, 374."

"Blake Street." I couldn't help frowning. "Don't you realize it's in a bad neighborhood?"

"I'd like to go there anyway," she insisted, tilting up her nose in a gesture I thought a little haughty. "A real poolroom, the kind you see in old movies. I think it might be interesting."

Interesting. I wondered if she knew the meaning of the

word. "Look, Carly, I don't want to spoil your fun, but it's not safe there, especially for a woman."

"But it's okay for a man?"

I wondered what kind of books she'd been reading lately. "I said *especially* for a woman. Believe me, it isn't the kind of place anybody goes for fun and recreation— any stranger, that is."

"According to who?"

I tried to pressure her. "Have you ever been in a pool hall? I mean a real, honest-to God smoke-filled rat hole crawling with human roaches who'd cut your throat for the change in your pocket?"

"Oh, my, there's that unmitigated faith in mankind again."

She was frustrating me to no end. "Okay, so I lean toward the dark side sometimes, and maybe they're not all quite that bad, I'll give you that. But I know reality and what I'm talking about, Carly. Take my word for it. I've been around, seen a lot. I think we should forget Willy's and go to the Metro. It's a clean place, modern, safe and in a good part of town."

"'Should.' Gosh, how I hate that word. It implies you have to live by somebody else's standards… You 'should' do this, or you 'shouldn't' do that."

"Rationalize all you like, Carly, but trust me, this is one 'should' you should listen to."

She swung toward me in her seat. "Bryan, if you're personally afraid, it's one thing. I can live with it. But if you don't want to take me because I'm a woman, that's another."

Damned right I was afraid for myself. Couldn't I already start to feel the sweat under my arms? But I didn't need to admit it. "I'm afraid, yes, afraid for you."

"Don't be, it's not necessary. Let's go."

Frustrated, I expelled a long breath. "I guess you're looking for an exciting new experience. Okay," I sang out, "if you're so determined ...." I jerked the wheel and swung right.

"Think of it as a sociology experiment," she said. "A learning experience."

More like a near-death experience, I thought. Or, worse, an actual death experience.

She smiled. "It's easy to be negative when you listen to all the hype on television, but worst case scenarios rarely turn out."

"Okay," I sighed, "I hear you; have it your way." I hoped she didn't hear me swallowing my voice.

It bothered the hell out of me the way she took such liberties with my feelings. I wished I could believe she felt that comfortable with me, that secure. It almost seemed like she was trying to drive me away. Or testing me, somehow. What I feared most is that I was being toyed with, that she was the cat and I the mouse.

Chapter 5

Blake Street. Once a bright avenue in a thriving business district, now a crime and rat- infested street littered with trash and broken glass, ground under the heels of poverty and neglect, a bleak and grimy street with heaved sidewalks and rank with the sour stink of rot and sewer gas, fronted by crumbling brick buildings webbed with graffiti, and boarded-up store fronts: a pawn shop and a used-furniture store— dark behind locked steel gates— and, across the street from a still-open liquor store, Willy's Pool Palace.

I pulled up several doors past the pool hall and parked under a street light.

"This is it," I said, intentionally ominous. "Look around. Take a good look. Do you want to change your mind?"

"It's a little drab, I'll admit," she said, glancing over her shoulder cautiously, "but you can't judge something by outward appearances alone. Really, it doesn't look nearly as bad as you made it out to be."

I snorted. Yes, I actually snorted. "Let's go, then," I said. "Don't lock it."

"Don't lock it?"

"Right, don't lock the door... and leave your purse here."

"In an unlocked car?"

"Shove it under the seat. You won't need it. Besides, we wouldn't want any of these upstanding citizens around here to think we don't trust them, do we?"

Before she could argue I slipped off my tie, unbuckled my seat belt and hustled around to her side of the car. I caught her hand as she stood up and escorted her past a few battered garbage cans lying askew on the ground, to the entrance to the pool hall. Together we stepped inside where the gloom swallowed us.

Heads turned.

Circled around three tables half a dozen characters resembling scarecrows draped on pool sticks peered from faces wreathed in smoke under undulating layers of blue haze. As many more characters sat crumpled in chairs along the wall, staring out of soulless eyes, like a Daniel Webster jury. The most prominent among them and glowering like the Devil himself, a man with a great beaked nose, broad forehead and coarse, long hair sat half-buried in a shaggy old army coat.

Gripping Carly's arm, I guided her toward a rack of pool cues standing like javelins against the wall behind the table nearest the entrance door. "Try a few and pick one that feels most comfortable," I said. "I'll get the cue ball and see if they have any soft drinks." I turned and ambled nonchalantly to the counter.

A slim black man with a polished bald head and polished fingernails gazed at me curiously out of soft, brown eyes, as if he was sizing me up.

"The table over there okay?" I asked, jerking a confident thumb.

"Number one, sure do," he drawled softly.

"Do you have anything to drink?"

"Only soft drinks," he replied, with a sly glance suggesting harder stuff could be had.

I pretended not to notice. "Make it two Cokes."

"No Coke, Pepsi do?"

"Fine," I said, leaning on the counter.

Keenly aware of the pungent reek of the place and the silence that had fallen since we came in, I glanced around, feigning interest in the game behind me: two players, one dark-skinned, goatee, acne-pitted; the other with surly eyes, ragged full beard and a greasy baseball cap.

"Two dolla's," the black man said, placing paper cups over the cans and sliding them over.

I dropped two singles on the counter. "Thanks..."

"Name's Willy."

"Thanks, Willy" I said, picking up the cans and cue ball and carried them back.

Carly had slipped out of her jacket and was comparing two sticks.

I set the bottles on a chair. "See if you can find a shorter one," I said, taking a stick down for myself and eyeing its length for straightness. "That one looks good for you, the one on your left." For the first time I saw how shapely she was: narrow waist blossoming into curvaceous hips down to gorgeous legs. An involuntary quiver shot through me.

I switched on the light above the table, feeling all the eyes on us, almost palpable, like fingers gently touching our bodies. I moved deliberately, trying not to let my agitation show. Nor my fear. Had I known beforehand where we were going, I would have brought a gun if I could have found one, or at least brought a pocket knife.

"Aren't you taking your jacket off?" she asked, sidling up to me.

My eyes fell briefly to her breasts, full under a salmon-colored blouse. *My God, unless it was the design of the bra, her nipples were protruding like bullets! And if I was seeing them, so was everyone else in the place.* "I'm all right for now," I said, feeling very angry at this obvious provocation, and ripping my eyes away as I racked the balls on the smooth green velvet bathed in a soft light. "We'll play straight pool, unless you prefer another game."

She tucked in her chin and smiled up guiltily. "How do you play it?"

Uh huh. Just as I thought, she knew nothing of the game and probably had never played on a pool table in her life. "Easy," I said, trying to hide the anger heating up my brain. "Just aim the cue ball at the ball you want to hit, and tell which pocket it's going into. Whoever sinks fifty balls first, wins. But we'll play to forty."

"All right, it sounds simple enough."

"Sure, nothin' to it. I'll break." Hunching over the table, I aimed and shot. The balls exploded around the table, bounding and rebounding softly off the cushions. "Bad break," I said, "nothing went in. Your turn." I pointed. "That eight ball near the corner is set to drop."

"I see it," she snapped, then softened instantly. "Thanks, but I'd like to figure it out for myself."

"Be my guest," I said, irked, and irked worse noticing the goatee and the baseball cap leering at her as she leaned in, angling the cue awkwardly across her thumb, her breasts brushing the edge of the table. They averted their eyes quickly when they saw me look over.

She let out a little squeal and turned to me, beaming. "I did it, I did it. The white ball went in with it, too. Does it count for two balls?"

I hated to spoil her delight. "It's called a scratch."

Her mouth turned down at the corners. "And that's not good?"

"It means you put the balls back on the table and lose your turn. It's okay, though. Since you're new at the game we won't count it."

She turned brittle. "We'll do no such thing, thank you. We'll go by the rules."

Shrugging, I retrieved the cue ball. "If you insist." I wondered if she'd let me save her if she was drowning.

Two newcomers barged through the door, balked at the sight of us, then shuffled past to join the two at the far end. Leading was a bruiser with a head that sat square on his shoulders, and wearing a thick wool sweater, a truck of a man with insolent eyes in a porky face, ruddy and smooth-shaven. From the bald spot on the crown of his flattish head flowed a curtain of straight, dirty-yellow hair, cut even across his upper back. Dragging behind, like an afterthought, scuffed the other, a slender frame under a leather jacket, hunched, with slits for eyes and a vulture's neck and face. To me, he looked stoned.

Growing more apprehensive by the minute, I chalked my cue stick and positioned myself between Carly and the curious eyes of those closest to us, gradually getting bolder. They seemed edgy and I could hear whispers passing between them.

The stick rode smoothly over my thumb and under the arch of my index finger, the good, familiar feeling of a sure and steady stroke. It had been years since I'd spent time in a pool hall, more time there than I cared to remember.

"That was terrific," she said, pressing close to my elbow. "How did you make the white ball come back so perfectly?"

Momentarily blinded by pride and warmed by the first kind thing she'd said all evening, I forgot my immediate fears. "If you hit the cue ball low, it'll spin backwards after it hits another ball. Don't you try it, though. If you tear the cloth with your stick this could turn into a costly game."

I sank three more balls before I missed.

She pointed overhead. "That must be how you keep score? By moving those beads along with your stick?"

"That's how it's done."

"You're so good," she said, with an admiring glance that for once didn't seem begrudged.

I swelled a bit. "I should have put the last one away, but I'm a little rusty."

Rusty, yes, I was, and damned nervous, too, with the jackals circling the table a few yards away. I couldn't concentrate. The unnatural calm, the thick mutterings out of the gloom unnerved me. At least I didn't hear swearing. What would I do then, remind them that there's a lady in the place? I worried. I had to think. The longer we stayed, the greater the danger. I could smell their intentions fouling the air.

Remembering her irritation, I said nothing when I saw her line up an impossible shot.

She pouted. "Oh, heck."

"You picked a tough one to go after," I said, chalking my stick and sizing up the table. I dropped in five more before missing.

"I should have suggested ping pong," she said, obviously piqued. "At least I'd have a chance to score a few points."

"I've had more practice than you. How about if I give you a handicap of, say, twenty? To sort of even things up."

"Thanks," she sniffed, "but no thanks."

I couldn't understand the perverse streak in her. What was so shameful about being taught or helped? Or was it because I'm a man? What was she trying to prove?

"Darn, another scratch. And the ball I hit didn't even go in the pocket."

"We all know what it feels like," I soothed, stepping up to the table. I ran the rest of the balls, racked them up again, broke the pack and dropped in three more before missing. "A good shot near the corner for you," I said, chancing her wrath.

Soft laughter from the far table made me jittery. At any given moment three of the four players at the end table were riveted on Carly, whether I was looking back at them or not. For sure, I didn't understand women very well, least of all her, but I darn sure did know men. I knew too well the lean and hungry look of sexual desire, the subtle agitations of yoked lust, the strained silence that grows out of dark concentration.

"I got it," she cried, hopping a little with delight. "Did you see it go in, right where I aimed?"

"Good shot," I said, watching from the corner of my eye the way the others prowled, languidly, and positioned themselves to get a closer, better view of her. "Go again." I saw the sweet curve of her lower body as she bent forward to shoot. And I knew they did, too.

What a fool I was to let her talk me into this! They wanted her, these dregs from Hell, salivated for her, and only I stood in their way. First they'd consider whether I brought her in to sell, or maybe to give her as a gift to satisfy some twisted need in myself. By now they knew neither was true. It wouldn't be long before they tested me in some way, probing for weakness, seeking vulnerability. They wouldn't make any radical moves at first, I knew, but with each failed attempt to get to her they would grow bolder, raise the ante on my nerves, escalate the danger until it would be too late to escape. I had to get her out of there. In a hurry. Do it while they were still disorganized and in a state of indecision. Do it before they could harden their resolve, close off the exits and take her. And I had no doubt they'd rape her, that they'd line up to take turns ravaging her on a pool table while I'd be pinned down to hear her screams, helpless to do anything about it!

Carly groaned her disappointment when she missed her shot.

Bitter and angry with myself, I stepped up beside her, determined to end the game and clear out before it was too late. I could only hope we still had time.

I kept my voice serious. "We have to get out of here right away," I said, lining up my shot.

She pouted. "Oh, sure, just when I'm catching on. It's early yet. We can play one more game, can't we? Unless you're afraid I'll beat you," she teased.

"It doesn't smell right to me in here. Something's going on." Keeping my face expressionless, I spoke in a harsh whisper. "I say we go. Go now!"

I know my face was stony with fear and concentration as I leaned over to take my shot. So naïve, so blind! How could she know so little about the world, about men. Even if she lacked experience, where the hell were her feminine instincts? Couldn't she sense the danger she was in, the mortal danger she was putting us both in!

Despite all the signs of danger around her, still Carly was naively unaware of what was happening. She had idealized this world, this subculture she regarded as merely a bunch of underprivileged people who would be just like herself if you treated them nicely and with respect. She believed they acted the way they do only because they felt left out, defeated and depressed. Maybe so. But what she didn't realize was this was a special kind of world, a hellish world its inhabitants could not see beyond, one that existed outside her theoretical utopia. The rules she lived by and thought were natural were foreign to the lost souls living here; the civility she took for granted and the values she embraced didn't apply to them. This was a world beyond her comprehension, where raw emotions ruled the mind and heart, a world of taking what you want however you can get it, a world of survival of the fittest, in its purest animal sense. It was a closed society of ruthless aggression, a place where innocence is doomed, and woe to the unfortunate stranger who wanders into it. Only the self matters here; everyone else be damned!

God how I wished I had a gun in my pocket!

Three splayed fingers steadied my hand on the table as my stick stroked evenly, once, twice, three times.

"Nice bank shot."

The voice came from over my right shoulder. A surge of adrenalin shot through me.

Straightening, I met the dead black eyes of the bruiser who had come in minutes ago, looking like Cochise, with his long hair and the headband he now wore.

"Just lucky," I said, calmly as I could.

"Lucky, hell." His mouth twisted in a sinister smile. "You made a few just like that one. Tough shots, all of them."

I pretended to size up the table. Just as I figured, it was starting. They were moving in, sounding me out. I took a quick glance at Carly, who was standing across the table, a picture of trust and innocence.

"How about you peel off the jacket and we have a game of nine-ball, you and me," Cochise said. "We could make it more interesting if you want to lay a couple of bucks on the line."

I leaned over for my shot. "Thanks, but we're leaving right after this game."

"Or how about this, a better idea. A game of partners. Far's I can see, your girlfriend here ain't had much chance against a shark like you. Say, you and Squint here against me and your girlfriend. Give her a chance to get some revenge. What about it, Pal?"

I could hardly see the table for the alarm bells blaring in my head. This intimidating mass of fat, bone and muscle was working me into a bind it might already be too late to squeeze out of.

"Thanks for the offer," I said, trying hard to veil my fear with a forced smile, "but—"

"Oh, Bryan, that sounds like fun."

I shot her a withering look that, had she seen it, would have stopped her heart.

"The lady says yes. That's good enough for me. Okay, man, you're on. Hey, Squint, set'm up, we're bumping heads again." He turned back and stuck out a meaty hand. "They call me Chief."

"Bryan," I said, squeezing against the crush of the grip I knew was gauging my will as well as his strength. "And she's Carly." I didn't miss the gloating, fat-lipped smile that flattened and spread Chief's nostrils, making him even uglier than he was.

"Carly, okay, Carly… and that's Squint with the busted nose."

Carly's 'Hi' came soft and subdued, and her eyes slid away, as if catching for the first time the scent of danger. She edged around closer to me.

"We'll play at this table," I said, determined to exert some control over the situation and our fate, Carly's and mine.

Chief stared at me a long moment, a hard, chilling stare that awakened fears in me I didn't know I had. "How come?" He bored in. "Squint's setting up the other table now."

"I feel comfortable here; I'm used to it. Besides," I said, speaking as boldly as I dared, "Squint can walk here easier than us three can walk there."

Chief nodded slowly, appraising me like some new species, obviously bewildered by my show of nerve. Or stupidity. "Hey, Squint." He waved over his shoulder. "On this table."

Carly whispered over to me. "Bryan, I'd like another drink if you don't mind."

Of all times to ask! I hated leaving her alone, even for a minute. "Okay, be right back," I said, picking up the empties. From the tail of my eye I saw Chief ogling her as he chalked the end of his cue stick.

"Two more," I said, my fingertips drumming the counter as I waited impatiently.

The black man slid the cold cans over with new cups and, head dipped, glanced around warily. "Two dolla's," he said, leaning forward and taking the bills. "Was I you, man" he whispered, "I'd buzz on out o' here in a haste."

I nodded and skirted the tables back to my own, convinced beyond doubt now that we were in great danger. Carly, her arms tight across her breast, had backed off a ways, with Chief at her side, talking into her ear. A few feet over from them, Squint leaned on his stick, his slim face and shoulders thrust forward.

I popped the can open, concentrating on keeping my hand

steady as I filled the cup and handed it to Carly.

"Straight pool okay with you?" Chief asked.

"Fine," I said, picking up my stick.

Chief gave me a hard look. "Take your coat off, why don'tcha, and make yourself at home."

"This is my lucky jacket."

Chief pulled a coin from his pocket and sent it twirling overhead. "Call it."

"Tails."

"Looks like that lucky jacket is off to a bad start for you. Okay, I break," he said, chalking his stick. "Hey, Squint, I'm counting on you to play your usual stinko game against my partner here." He winked at Carly and spoke out the side of his mouth. "Squint's the nervous type, gets rattled easy."

Squint sneered. "Worry about yourself, Chief."

Chief was good, very good. In no time at all he had run the score up almost double mine and Squint's. I wondered whether Squint was as bad as he looked, or whether he was throwing the game because he was scared of Chief. Carly managed to sink a couple of balls and was beginning to relax and smiled whenever her partner made a shot.

Chief stepped up as Carly was about to shoot and spread his meaty hand over hers. "Like this, honey," he said, shaping her fingers on the table. He wrapped his hand around hers.

I glared, but only Squint seemed to notice, and maybe that murderer's row, too, squatting along the side, with the shaggy-coat Satan at their head, sitting propped against the wall.

"Now draw the stick back straight," Chief breathed in her ear, "nice and easy. Let it slip through your fingers, slip nice and easy, don't squeeze... that's right... you're getting it... stroke even, back and forth... get the rhythm...back and forth." He stepped back, leering. "Do it a couple of times till you get the feel of it good, then let it go."

I stood watching helplessly, listening to his filthy innuendos. Didn't Carly recognize his words for what they were? I could feel rage boiling my blood. She resented my holding a door open for her, yet here she stood letting this lowland gorilla practically make obscene love to her. At the same time my heart ached with worry. This was already getting way out of hand. I was being tested, I knew, to see how much I would tolerate, to see how far they could push me, to determine what it would take to get me out of the picture.

Carly gave a little whoop as her ball dropped in the pocket.

"Good shot, partner," Chief said, patting her back and giving it a little extra rub. "Let's see you do it again." He cozied up to her. "There's a good shot along the cushion. This is tricky. Let me show you the best way on this one." He looped his arm around her back as she leaned over the table and grasped her elbow. "Don't go side to side here. Pump smooth."

There, he did it again with his mouth and I had to take it.

Carly shot. "Darn it. I missed."

"Don't worry, partner, you did great." He lit up a cigarette and blew a plume of smoke off to the side. "Hey, Carly, we make a beautiful team."

Squint took his shot and missed.

"You got a good eye, Squint," Chief taunted. "Why don't you take it out and wash it sometime." His harsh laugh held no trace of warmth or humor.

There was no way I could hide my sour face as I stepped in after Chief. I had to think and think fast to get Carly and myself out of this spot. By now everyone in the joint was watching us, I knew, watching and waiting for the action that was bound to happen soon. A curious mixture of tension and excitement filled the air. Even Willy, his smooth pate bobbing behind the counter as he went about his chores, glanced up apprehensively from time to time to watch the unfolding drama. I hadn't for a second forgotten his warning, *Was I you I'd buzz on out of here in a haste.* Chalking my stick, I squatted to eye a shot. Despite the knots in my stomach I managed to run the rest of the rack.

Impressed, Chief nodded. "You're okay, man. Maybe after this you and me can go head to head."

My concentration broken, I flubbed my next shot and stepped back. Next up, across the table, Carly flashed me a warm smile. I felt oddly reassured.

I noticed then, for at least the second time since we'd begun playing, that Squint was leaning on me, literally leaning his weight against me and forcing me to move. This time I didn't fail the test. I wrapped my arm around him, took a sudden step backward and caught Squint's shoulders as he lurched sideways in front of me.

"Your turn, Squint," I said, feigning innocence and giving him a friendly shove. "She missed."

A stifled squawk escaped Squint's throat as he recovered his balance.

Chief turned his sweat-greased face to him. "Whatsa matter, Squint, can't you stand the pressure?" He laughed. "Or can't you stand, period?"

Squint's slitted eyes fixed him with a mixed look of pain and anger. "You're a riot, Chief. A real life-of-the-party comedian."

Chief swung to me. "Hey, what an idea! How 'bout it, we

make a party, just us four. 'Less Squint don't want to go. He ain't much fun anyway." He scanned our faces. "How's it sound? Over to my digs. Got some good stuff, top shelf— Jack Daniels, Chivas Regal. Nothing but the best. Beefeaters gin, if you like something like that, Carly. We can talk, get to know each other better. Got some good rap music, too. What do you say?"

"We have other plans," I said, putting a hard edge to my voice. "Thanks anyway."

Chief glowered. "Other plans?" He nodded slowly, as if needing time to digest my words, then turned to Carly. "How 'bout it, partner, what do *you* say?"

Carly shied away from his cold eyes. "No, we really do have to go."

He swung around scowling. "Hey, Willy, pour me my usual." He snatched up his stick. "Come on, Squint, goddamit, get the hell out of the way so I can shoot!"

I could see at last that Carly was waking up to the danger facing us. I saw, too, how Chief could only get nastier now that he'd been openly rebuffed. And if he started drinking more than he obviously already did, who could say what he'd do next.

Chief flubbed his shot, muttered a soft curse and shambled off to the counter for his drink.

I saw him down a couple of quick swallows and stick his glass out to Willy for a refill.

"One for me, too, Willy," Squint called in a warbly voice. He stood an uncertain moment, watched me sink a shot and scuffled away.

I intentionally missed my next shot so I could get close to Carly as she stepped in nervously to shoot. Up to that moment Chief had kept himself solidly planted between us, apparently to keep us from talking privately and maybe to see how far he could get with Carly himself.

"Take this," I whispered, smiling around innocently when I said it. Secretly, I pressed the ignition key into her hand. "When I say go, you go. Don't wait, don't ask questions, don't think, just do it! Get out fast as you can and start the car. Be ready to peel out."

Her eyes shone with misty regret. Or fear. Or both. She knew now she was blood in the water to these sharks and that they were circling tighter by the minute.

Chief was growling something to Squint that I couldn't quite hear.

"Don't forget, Carly, fast!" I whispered sharply as I watched Squint hustle back with Chief at his heels. "Be ready to floor it. If I don't get to you in time, don't worry about me, just get yourself the hell out of here."

She looked like she was about to protest, when Chief strode up to the table.

"Hotshot missed, I see," he mocked, setting his drink aside and looking up at the score.

"Yeah, Squint was a little off the mark," I said, intentionally misunderstanding.

We played around the table a few times. Chief missed an easy shot and Squint laughed, a dry, cackling laugh. "What's the matter, Chief, losing your magic touch?"

Chief hauled his huge bulk upright and brought a menacing face close to Squint's twitching mouth. "How 'bout I touch you with these," he snarled, fingering his callused knuckles, "and make your face disappear?"

Willy's voice wafted over softly. "Le's keep it peaceful, you boys. I don' want no po-lice coming down on my place. Got 'nough troubles," he trailed off.

"Yeah, sure, Willy, no problem." Chief's thick finger twanged across Squint's nose. The snap brought instant, involuntary tears to Squint's eyes, but he took the pain stoically, without making a sound or even flinching.

Chief smirked, obviously unimpressed with Squint's bravado. He picked up his drink, took a slug and turned suddenly on me. "What're you smiling about?"

I felt the blood drain from my face. "Who's smiling?"

"And what're you two doing down here anyway? You don't live around here."

"We're...visiting. Is anything wrong with that?"

"Visiting. Like at the zoo, is that it? Come to see the animals?"

A cold sweat was beginning to trickle down my chest. My eyes burned in the smoky air that hovered over the room like a blue cloud. My heart thumped with a rhythm to match my racing brain. Chief's drinking was catching up to him now and with a loosening of control he was becoming more aggressive and dangerous. Carly saved the moment. "Bryan, I'm going to get my make-up out of the car. I'll be back in a minute."

Chief grabbed her arm as she turned to go. "You don't need it, babe, you look great like you are." He looked around. "Don't she, you guys?"

I couldn't hold back. "Get your hands off her!"

Chief swelled before me like some beast inflating itself, welcoming the challenge he had instigated. "And who's gonna make me?" he asked, an ugly grin on his face.

"I am," I said, my words forced out of my throat as tight as

75

my hand on my cue stick.

Out of the gloomy shadows along the wall, like the Devil himself, materialized the shaggy coat. Tall, angular, with a heavily-boned face and bulgy eyes, hard and cold as billiard balls, he spoke with total conviction, like a man used to giving orders and having them obeyed.

"Is this how we treat visitors to our neighborhood?"

Chief's hand fell to his side. "Yeah, sure, Hinch—I mean no, no we don't."

"We have to show hospitality, don't you see? Otherwise people get the wrong impression. It gives us a bad reputation." He exhaled a plume of cigar smoke. "You understand, Chief?"

"Yeah, I get it, Hinch. I see your point."

"Good, very good." He tapped the ashes off his cigar. "Now apologize to the lady."

"Hey, Hinch—"

With thick brows knitted, the big man clenched the cigar between his teeth. "She's waiting."

Head low, Chief shuffled his feet. "Hey, I'm sorry, okay? No harm intended."

To Carly, Hinch said, "Chief forgets his manners every so often, especially when he's had a couple of drinks. I have to remind him. He's all right when he's sober and not a bad guy when you get to know him." He turned back to Chief. "So? You going to stand there all day with your mouth open catching flies? Go tell Willy to break out the good stuff he hides under the counter. Top shelf for our guests. And tell him to lock the door. We'll have a get-acquainted party right here. By the looks of it he won't be getting any more business tonight, anyway."

"Sure, Hinch. Gottcha."

I didn't miss the quick exchange between them. Not a smile, exactly, but a dumb grin from Chief, and from Hinch, a corrosive, mirthless parting of thick lips that exposed his horsey teeth.

The darting glance I got from Carly told me she understood: Hinch, sounding very much like a decent, even intelligent, man riding in like a hero to save them from danger, but in reality the greater menace.

"You guys," Hinch said, snapping his fingers to the crew along the wall, "you guys don't have an invite. You're stinking up the place and you don't spend a buck all night between the lot of you. Willy's not running a welfare office here. Take a hike, beat it, scram. And don't be hanging around outside attracting any cop's attention."

Lethargically they rose, groaning their disappointment, and filed past with the hopeless dejection of a Georgia chain gang. A few hung back, dragging their feet, probably hoping for a reprieve.

"Monk, I owe you, so you can stay," he said to the hairy-faced sloth at the far end.

"I'm staying, too, ain't I, Hinch?" Squint said, lining up a shot.

"I'm not chasing you out, am I?"

I was about to give the signal when Carly spoke up. "Now may I get my make-up from the car?" She said it boldly, not like one asking permission. "After all, I want to look my best if we're having a party here."

Hinch smiled a gruesome smile. "Sure, you're my special guest tonight. I want you to shine for the boys." He reached out and stroked her face. "And I want to personally make you happy." His tongue curled slowly over his lips. "Very happy."

77

Carly recoiled from his obvious intent and burning eyes.

As she started for the side he spoke again. "Leave your coat, you don't need it.... Squint," he indicated with a toss of his head, "you go, too. Make sure nothing happens to her." He turned to me. "Insurance, in case any of those waste products are still outside and try to give her trouble."

Despite Hinch's warning, they could still be lurking around anywhere nearby, I thought, but I hoped not. I nodded in Carly's direction, praying that she was paying close attention. I saw her edge back, ready to make her break.

"Ah, hell, Hinch," Squint whined, watching the ball kiss off another and go astray. "She ain't goin' no place, not with her boyfriend still here."

"I said go with her!"

Seeing Willy skirt the counter with Chief and head toward the door to lock it, I crossed to the far end of the table alongside Squint. "Here, Squint," I said, giving him a hard shove, "I'll show you how to make a shot like that."

"Hey, man, wait a fuckin'—"

"Squint, go do what I said," Hinch ordered. "Now!"

"What is it with you, man?" Squint said, pushing back against me. "Hey, let go my fuckin' stick."

I collared him and pulled him in close. "I think you've been throwing this game, Squint, that's what I think."

"What the—"

I snatched the stick away and shoved him back full force, toppling Hinch as he tumbled against his legs.

"Go!" I yelled to Carly, "Go!"

Taking the narrow end of the stick I slammed the thick end

against Squint's head, brought it back and with full strength brought it down like a sledge hammer on Hinch's neck. Backing away, I twirled it over his head like a helicopter propeller before slinging it toward Chief, already rushing toward me. It caught Chief across the face and he stumbled back, taking Willy down with him.

I hurled myself across the table, scooped up an armful of balls and backed toward the door, firing at their heads as I went. I was stepping over Hinch to get to through the doorway when I felt the clamp of Hinch's powerful hand around my ankle as he tried to pull himself off the floor.

Hinch growled. "That sweet cunt is going to be mine, you sonofabitch. Mine, you understand? And you're going to watch me fuck her to death."

With a couple of balls left and with all the power I could muster, I smashed one alongside Hinch's head. "Fuck you, too," I said, hearing his skull crack as I tore his hand free and drove my foot into his groin.

I heard Hinch's deathly groan as I fired the last two balls. One nailed Chief between the eyes just as he rose from the floor and leaped toward me, skewing his lunge. I didn't see what or who the other ball hit because I was already turned and out the door, where I pivoted and broke into a frantic run, tripping over a garbage barrel, with my soles slipping and scraping on the cement.

"Go!" I cried out, "Go!" My heart and feet pounded together.

Tearing the car door open, I glanced back and saw bodies spilling out of the poolroom onto the sidewalk, with Chief between them, bellowing.

"Come on, dammit," I cried, jumping into the passenger seat, "come on!"

Panic shrilled her voice. "I can't get the key in. It's stuck!"

"It's upside down!" I reached over, jerked it free, jammed it in right and turned it. "Hit it!" I cried, seeing three or four of them framed in the rear window, their long hair flying and coming fast. I threw myself back and slapped the door lock.

The engine roared to life, tires screaming on the pavement at the same time Chief's distorted face slammed up against the window, his hand tearing at the door handle.

Looking back, I saw him sprawled on the curb along with someone else under the street light as we burned away, fishtailing down the block....

"Okay," I said, after traveling a short distance, panting and still trying to catch my breath, "we're all right now.... Slow down... slow down... before we kill ourselves."

She eased up on the pedal. "Look, my hand is shaking," she said, holding it out.

I took her hand in mine. "Cold as ice. Mine's hot."

She shuddered. "Bryan, I can't believe this, I can't believe this."

"You'd better pull over... let me take the wheel now."

She pulled up to the curb and we got out to change places. We started out again and she reached over.

"Bryan..."

I took her hand again.

"Thanks...thanks for—"

"Squint threw that game, I swear it," I said, still breathing hard and wiping sweat from my forehead. "We really should have won the game."

Neither of us said anything for a minute or so. "Bryan, do you think they really…I mean, is it possible…?"

I gazed into her innocent blue eyes. "What, that they were serious? Heck, no. They were just a weird bunch of underprivileged souls, victims of our unjust society, having a little fun at our expense. Do you want to go back and get your coat?"

She gave me a quick look I didn't want to interpret.

After a few moments she said, "Maybe a Tennessee Williams' play wouldn't have been so bad after all."

Tonight will be more memorable than any Williams play ever would be. "So, how about a cup of coffee?"

"I could use something stronger than coffee, but okay."

Chapter 6

Carly sat rigid, using two slightly trembling hands to hold the cup to her lips. "Well," she said faintly, "are you going to say it, or do I have to say it for you?"

"What's that?"

"'I told you so.'"

I shrugged. "Actually, you were right, nothing happened."

"Nothing happened! Those vicious guys were ready to kill, and you say nothing happened? Especially the one who looked like a bearded pirate."

"Hinch."

"Yes, him, Hinch. At least Chief, awful as he was, had emotions… seemed partly human. But the other one, my God— how did you ever get out of that death trap alive?"

"Me?" I set my cup down. "I just told them I had to get up early for work and excused myself."

She smiled wryly. "Of course, and they came dashing out to escort you home."

"No, actually they wanted me to stay. They liked me so much they couldn't bear to part company and see me leave."

"At least not with your life." She shuddered. "Really, Bryan, you almost didn't. We almost didn't."

"I know…how about some eggs or pancakes?"

"Thanks, but I'm not the least bit hungry."

I glanced at the menu. "I think I'll have a piece of pie."

"Bryan, how can you eat? My stomach is doing flip-flops and I'm still shaking. Look," she said, holding out her hand.

"I have to keep my energy up, don't I? Never know when I might have to run the fifty yard dash again."

"I'm sorry, Bryan. It's all my fault. If only I hadn't been so insistent on going there, none of this would have happened." She laid her hand on mine.

Seeing her so tender made me want to reach over and take her in my arms. "No harm done." In fact, seeing her so gentle and warm, it almost seemed worth the danger. "Except of course you're out a jacket," I said, signaling the waitress. Unless you want to go back and try talking them into returning it."

"Bryan, that really is not funny."

The waitress came up to take my order. "Sure you won't have something to eat, Carly?" I pressed. She shook her head. "Okay," I said, looking up, "one piece of cherry pie."

Carly fidgeted with her napkin. "The more I think of it, the scarier it gets. You could have been hurt."

Right, I thought, like someone caught in a threshing machine is 'only' hurt. "Black eyes and broken bones heal, Carly. It's you I was worried about. There's no imagining what fate awaited you."

"I understand. Thanks," she said softly, picking at her napkin.

How lovely—no, how *gorgeous* she was, sitting across from me, so demure, so vulnerable. Alluringly sad, too, with her hair a little disheveled and pasted to her still-damp brow, her skin flushed, the gloss eaten from her tender lips.

"You knew something like this would happen, didn't you?"

I tried to look surprised. "I did?"

"Don't lock the door…"

"Oh, that. I was hoping the car would be stolen so I could collect the insurance. I could use a new car." My feeble bid for a smile failed.

"I guess you must think I'm pretty dumb."

"Putting words in my mouth? It never entered my mind."

"No, but you must think it."

"I may think you're naive in some ways, maybe, but not dumb. Or maybe a little too trusting. I think I happen to know this city a little better than you do."

The waitress set down the pie and lifted the pot. "Warm it up?" she asked, pouring before I could answer.

"Bryan, I know tonight was a mistake, a terrible mistake, but I also believe it was a freakish thing. We just happened to pick a place with a bunch of jerks in it."

"It's places like that where jerks live. It's their habitat," I said, speaking over the pie balanced on my fork. "What's that Chinese proverb? 'He who make mistake and not learn from it make two mistakes.'"

"You're glad this happened, aren't you?" she said, suddenly peevish. "Glad to prove me wrong."

"Believe me, Carly, nothing could be further from the truth."

"The truth, yes. You have yours and, in spite of tonight, I have mine."

Not again, I thought. "And never the twain shall meet?"

"Now who's putting words in whose mouth?"

That strange familiarity again. Why did she feel she could antagonize me this way without driving me off? Or was that her intention? I rankled again remembering how she let that slob nuzzle up to her ear, hold her hand on the table and even wrap his arm around her waist, showing her how to shoot. Why, I'd seen more fear in her eyes when I offered to help with her tire the first time we met. My blood pressure rose thinking about it, and remembering, too, how she manipulated me by suggesting I was afraid. I averted my eyes so I wouldn't have to look at her.

She rested her chin on her laced fingers. "You're angry."

Again that amused smile. Playing with my feelings, toying with me, obviously gave her a perverse kind of pleasure. "How about more coffee?" I said, ignoring her remark.

"You're angry because I got us into this, aren't you?"

"It's not your fault. As I said, you weren't aware of the risk."

"I know," she said, half apologetically.

I looked at her doubtfully, wondering how long I could ride this emotional roller coaster she had me on.

"I may be dumb about some things, Bryan. Lisa says I am, but I'm not a complete fool. It took me awhile to catch on, true, and even then I wasn't sure because basically I trust people and believe in always giving others the benefit of a doubt, but when that smelly- breath Chief whispered in my ear I should get rid of you and…something else, I knew we were in trouble."

"And he got ticked when you refused."

"I didn't exactly refuse him. I didn't want to make him suspicious, so I told him, as nicely as I could— my skin was crawling— I said we had to be somewhere else, but we could make a date for tomorrow. I guess he didn't believe me."

"Guys like that don't take rain checks."

"I didn't want to antagonize him, once I knew what he was up to, so... I played along."

Very well, too, I thought, well enough to fool me. I wasn't quite sure I could buy her whole story; she could have been covering up for her own gullibility. She might even have been unconsciously attracted to the animal vibes. Some women are like that. But her answer was enough to satisfy me, at least for the time being.

"Bryan, think of it as a learning experience, something I can use for a class project." She brightened. "This could be a blessing in disguise. I could develop a thesis based on it. A social experiment."

Sure, I thought, one that could have made statistics out of us. At the same time, I realized, sharing danger seemed to have softened her defenses, had brought us a little closer together. Maybe even won a little appreciation for myself.

"A hard-earned experience that won't soon be forgotten," I said, seeing again that devilish glint in her eyes.

She covered her mouth to stifle a giggle.

I felt a twinge of discomfort. "You want to share the joke?"

"I'm sorry," she said, "but if you could have seen yourself... the way I did in the rear-view mirror while I was trying to start the car... flying out the door with your arms flapping... like Big Bird on Sesame Street...."

Embarrassed, I bowed my head. There I was, hoping my heroics impressed her, and all she could recall was a grotesque caricature of me like a big turkey fleeing for its life.

Her giggle, her laugh, was infectious, though, and I began to see the humor in it and laughed with her, softly at first, then, despite ourselves, louder until every head in the place had turned to stare at what must have seemed to be a man and a woman who were mentally unbalanced.

The tension broken between us made it seem suddenly all was right with the world. We talked, and while we were talking, I determined that tonight, yes, before this very hour was out, I would take her in my arms and kiss her, crush those lush and tender lips to mine until she could no longer breathe.

"You must be getting chilly without a jacket," I said. "Shall we go?"

Chapter 7

"Well," Lisa said, eyeing me up and down, "will you look at what the cat dragged in?"

I flopped on the bed. "I look worse than I feel."

"I'm glad of that." Hauling herself up to a squat position on the bed, Lisa plopped her pillow on her lap and cocked her head. "But you'd never guess it by the looks of you. What happened, did you find out he's an animal and have to fight him off?"

"No, nothing like that, believe me."

"Well what then, for gosh sakes? Where'd he take you, to a dog fight? I don't blame you for not inviting him inside."

"He took me to a poolroom."

"A poolroom? Carly, you've got to be kidding. Couldn't he do any better than that? A poolroom! Doesn't he have any class at all?"

I giggled. "It was my idea."

Lisa's green eyes rolled up. "You know, Carly, you really are loony tunes. And he must be the same to go along with your nutty ideas. I think you're losing it more than ever, I honestly do, especially the way you've been acting lately." She tossed her head. "Now me and David, that's different. After going out with him for dinner— no cheap place either— I know what it means to be treated decently, with respect."

"So why are you back so early?"

Lisa hesitated. "He had a phone call. An important matter, he said, so he brought me home."

"Business?"

Lisa looked annoyed and uncomfortable. "I don't know. He didn't say and I didn't ask. I didn't want him to think I was being nosy. Sticking your nose into other people's business makes you sound distrustful and causes trouble. Getting along is based on trust. I trust David and I think that's why we...we harmonize together."

"Harmonize. Really?"

"Yes, really. You and Bryan should double-date with us sometime and see for yourself. Maybe you could both learn something— and I'm not saying that to be insulting, Carly, or to get even for what you said about him. To put it bluntly, Carly, he's mature, and it's more than I can say for you and Bryan boy, at least from what you just told me."

"Fine."

"Fine? Is that all you can say, fine?"

"I mean fine. Set up a date."

Lisa's jaw dropped. "Do you mean it?"

"Do I have to put it in writing and have it notarized?"

Lisa looked askance. "This isn't one of your clever tricks, is it, Carly?"

"Why, Lisa, darling, whatever do you mean?"

"I mean to watch me like a big sister, or maybe to try to figure out some theory on David and use it against him to break us up."

"Lisa, it was your idea, remember?"

"Yes, well..."

"Besides, if what you say is true for you, then it's true the other way around for me." I got up and went to the dresser for my things while Lisa mulled over my words. "I'm going to soak in the tub now, Lisa," I said, heading for the bathroom, "so why don't we drop the subject for now."

Anxious to get rid of the stale- smoke smell of my clothes, I turned on the faucet and disrobed. Lisa called over the roar of the tub water. "Carly...? Carly, where's your jacket? Did you forget it in Bryan's car?"

"I donated it for a worthy cause."

"What?"

I opened the door a crack and stuck my face out. "Actually, I exchanged it for my virginity."

Lisa hurled her pillow against the bathroom door. "Goodnight, Carly!"

Chapter 8

The morning after the fiasco at Willie's Poolroom, I stood outside my shower drying myself, thinking of Carly and the last few minutes we spent together the evening before in the vestibule of her apartment. I was holding her hands, looking deep into her eyes, feeling tense and embarrassed as I searched for the right words to touch her heart. I had just mustered enough courage to pull her into my arms and kiss her, when Lisa's voice called from behind the door.

"Carly, is that you?"

"Yes, it is, Lisa."

"Somebody's with you?"

"Yes, it's Bryan."

"Hi, Bryan."

"Hi," I answered, "hi, Lisa."

"Are you coming in with him, Carly? 'Cause if you are I have to put some clothes on."

"Don't bother, Lisa. Bryan's leaving now."
She slipped neatly away from my outstretched arms and out of my jacket. "I'm sorry," she said, handing my jacket back to me."

Lisa broke the spell and it irked me. I stammered, "Is it okay then if I call you in a couple of days?"

"Sure. You might have to try a couple of times to reach me, but I'd like that."

"And you have my home and cell numbers, in case you need to call me for any particular reason. There on the napkin?" I said, not quite knowing how to break it off.

She patted her purse. "I have it right here."

"Good," I said, shuffling back toward the outside door. "I'll be in touch."

"Bryan....?"

"Yes?"

"It wasn't so bad, was it? I mean…"

"It was fun." In the ghostly light of the hallway I saw the shine of her misty eyes and the glimmer of a sad smile.

"Thanks… and Bryan?"

"Yes?"

"I lied. I never played pool before yesterday."

I reached for the doorknob. "Really? Now *that* I don't believe. But there is one thing, though, I've been wondering about all evening."

"What is it?"

"If you could have got the ignition key in straight, would you still have waited for me?"

She smiled. "Now that's something you'll never know, will you…?"

* * * * *

Hearing my cell phone ringing, I hurried out of the bathroom to answer it. "Hello."

"Hi, sweetie. Guess who?"

My heart fell. "Hello, Cindy."

"Oh, my, don't we sound thrilled."

"It's been a while."

"Oh, so you noticed."

A long, deadly silence fell between us.

"So what are you doing?" she asked.

"Standing here shivering, talking to you, with a bath towel wrapped around me."

"Hmmmm, sounds interesting."

"Did you want something, Cindy?"

"Well, thank you very much. You don't call in a month—a month and two days to be exact, then when *I* call *you,* you ask what I want."

"I've been rushing around here, getting ready to leave."

"Too busy to return my calls and find out if I'm living or dead?"

She had an annoying way of putting me on the defensive. "Things have been pretty hectic lately. Look, Cindy, I've been on the go day in and day out. Either I'm in court or working on motions or talking with clients…. I don't have any time to waste and I'm not in the mood for any of this. If there's something special—"

"'Any time to waste?' Is that what you call it? Well, listen, sweetie, don't you think I'm busy, too, with a company to run? I've got people hounding me all day with problems and questions. A thousand decisions to make, and I still find time to call you. I don't consider it a waste because—"

"Cindy," I said, trying to be patient, "I hope you didn't call to start another argument. I'm not up to—"

"So I'm to blame. Is that what you're saying? *I'm* the one who starts all the arguments? Well, isn't that ironic! I go out of my way, take time off from my friends— yes, I do have friends, in case you forgot or didn't know— and stay home waiting for you to call, and you accuse me—"

I held my phone away from my ear, waiting for her to run out of breath:

Good old Cindy, I thought, always on the go, ambitious and searching for excitement whenever she could get away from her work as a chief executive with HiLite Cosmetics. On the job she could be deadly serious, a driven, dominating force, but when she wasn't working, she loved going to places with music that shook the walls, loved to dance and flaunt her wicked body until guys' tongues hung down to the floor. At first I didn't mind; in fact, I enjoyed the wild times, the attention she brought us, all the sexually-charged excitement of living the fast life, even when it left me bleary-eyed on those mornings when I had to get to the office or court early.

But somewhere along the way I lost interest in the whole scene. The noise, the crowds, the phony good times all seemed to catch up to me at once. And along with my disenchantment with the life I was leading came a loss of interest in Cindy. My feelings for her— if they had ever been anything more than infatuation and (I had to be honest with myself) a crazy, sexual attraction— just seemed to fade. How the change in me came about I didn't know. It just happened, suddenly, as if I woke up one morning a different person. But Cindy hadn't changed, and she couldn't accept the change in me or our circumstances.

"All right, Cindy, all right," I said, cutting off her diatribe. "Shall we start again?"

Her voice softened. "I just want you to know you're not the

only one with feelings Bryan."

"I know that."

"The truth is, honey, I've missed you terribly."

Silence.

"So? Aren't you going to say you missed me, too?"

"Look, Cindy, don't get upset now, but I thought— I mean, after our last time together we agreed to break off for a while. Remember?"

"Of course I remember. We were mad at each other, although I can't remember exactly what about and I'll bet you can't, either. But, honey, everybody has arguments and say things they don't mean."

"I still think we should hold off for a while. All we seem to do lately is fight when we're together and frankly I'm tired of it. I don't need the grief."

"You're tired of it, and I suppose I love it."

I wanted to tell her that she seemed to thrive on it. "All I'm saying is that if we have to end every date with hard feelings, it isn't worth it."

"You mean I'm not worth it. Is that it? First you say talking to me is a waste of time and now you're telling me I'm not worth it. Is that what you're saying, Bryan? Did I get it right?"

"See what I mean? We can't carry on a civil discussion without fighting. I'm saying enough is enough."

"Go ahead, blame it on good old Cindy. It's her fault, it's always her fault, never your fault."

"Cindy, listen to me. Put the blame where you want, but I think we need a breather from each other. I need time alone and I'm sure you do, too. Just some time to let the waters calm. You agreed to it. Why can't we just leave it that way for now? Maybe in a month or so—"

"A month or so! How could you? After all we've done together." Her voice turned sultry. "After all we've meant to each other? Did you forget…."

Cindy, valentine-heart face and lips, warm cocoa-brown eyes, hair streaked honey-gold. Cindy, bubbling with energy and anticipation, an uninhibited spirit embracing life and seeking pleasure wherever she went. Cindy, affectionate, tender, wrapping her arms around my waist, pushing herself tight against me and gazing up to me with an insatiable hunger born deep in her soul.

And later, as I began to cool toward her, a different Cindy emerged: tempestuous and volatile and possessive, capricious as the emotional winds that buffeted her heart, ever more spiteful and vindictive.

"Are you listening to me, Bryan? I'm *talking* to you."

"Of course I'm listening."

"Well, you could be a little more responsive. Anyway, I didn't forget any of it, Bryan, not a minute of all the time we spent together—going out dancing or to the beach, the partying, the love—"

"Cindy, don't. It's not as if I didn't enjoy any of those times together, because I did. They meant a lot to me and—"

"Then let's forget this stupid agreement, as you call it, and see each other! It's been too long already." Her voice softened. "I really miss you, honey. I need you. You don't know how much."

I let out a long sigh. I really didn't want to hurt her, she meant a great deal to me at one time, but that was the past and this was now. I had to make her understand. "Cindy, no, let's not. Not yet, anyway." I could visualize her face frosting over.

"Okay, Bryan, now let's have the real reason."

"You know the reason. I just told you the reason."

"No, I don't know the reason, not the real reason. You're not kidding me, Bryan. I wasn't born yesterday. You've been looking for an excuse to break up for a long time. I could feel it coming for… for months. If you're worried that I'm looking for a wedding ring, forget it. For your information, sweetie, I wouldn't marry you for all the coffee in South America."

"Cindy, I told you—"

"You told me crap. What's her name, do I know her? One of my so-called good friends?"

"Whose name do you want me to give you?"

She exploded. "Don't play dumb! There's another girl in the picture. I sense it. A woman has a way of knowing such things."

Of course she was right, more right than she could possibly know. But there was no other girl involved when I first tried to break off the relationship. None at all. "Cindy, you're making things up."

"Oh, I see, now I'm imagining things." Her voice dripped sarcasm. "I'm paranoid is that it? Is that what you're trying to say?"

"Believe what you want, Cindy. I give up. I'm through trying to explain."

"Well, if you think I'm going to wait around until you're ready to see me, you need a snug-fitting straight jacket. You're not the only apple on the tree. Just forget us completely, the past, present and future!"

"We don't have to be enemies, Cindy. I don't want hard

feelings between us. We've been friends too long."

She scoffed. "Friends."

"Yes, at least we can stay friends."

"Go to hell!"

I winced, sensing her thumb pressing a hole in her off button as the line went dead. I rubbed my ear. What a woman! What a temper! She must eat gunpowder for breakfast. Never had I met anyone like her in my life. I opened my dresser drawer and took out a fresh pair of shorts and socks. I was half-dressed when my phone rang again.

"Hello."

"Bryan, I'm sorry I hung up on you like I did, but I was upset. Did you think it over?"

"Think what over, Cindy?"

Again, the same sensation of violent anger and frustration as the phone went dead. I had just slipped my tie under my collar when the phone rang a third time.

"Hello."

"Bryan, you are a dirty bastard!" And yet again, another angry hang-up.

Thirty seconds later the ringing phone jangled my nerves.

I barked, "What now!"

"Excuse me...Bryan?"

"It is," I said, cooling quickly. "Who's this?"

"It's Carly. Don't you recognize my voice?"

I stood there half-stunned. "Carly."

"Carly Miller, remember me? With the flat tire? The pool

hall queen?"

"Carly, sure. I didn't expect you to— you caught me off guard."

"I guess so. You almost bit my head off."

"Sorry, but I had a couple of cranky calls a few minutes ago."

"You mean crank calls."

"'Cranky' is still the word."

"Anyway, I hope I'm not calling too early or at an inconvenient time."

"No, not at all...is everything all right?"

"Oh, yes, fine. I just wanted to save you the trouble and let you make other plans for this weekend. In case you were thinking of calling, that is."

My heart dropped. Was this Carly's way of easing me out of her life? Was she doing to me what I'd been doing do Cindy? "Okay," I said, keeping my voice steady. "No problem. I had plans for this weekend anyway. Maybe I'll run into you again sometime."

"I won't be busy forever," she said. "Right now I need every available minute to work on my term papers. I wasn't thinking too clearly last night. But what I want to ask is, are you free next Tuesday, about twelve noon?"

"Tuesday?" I repeated, taken somewhat aback. "I guess I can work my time around. What did you have in mind, lunch?"

"Let's keep it a surprise, shall we?"

"Oh, no."

She laughed. "Not like the last one, I promise."

"I hope not because I can't stand the sight of blood. Especially my own."

"What a funny thing to say."

"Funny now," I said, "but it wasn't then. You want me to pick you up at your place?"

"I think it would be out of the way. Do you know where the Jamison fire house is?"

"It's only a few miles from here, yes."

"Meet me in the parking lot there. Twelve sharp?"

"Twelve sharp it is."

"Great. I have to go now. We're getting busy and I have customers waiting."

"Oh, you're at work?"

The phone clicked.

I hung up, trying to visualize the Jamison area: a big Sears store anchoring a shopping center a block away from the fire house. Continental Bowlodrome. A Borders bookstore... or was it Media Play? A Thai restaurant and a couple of chain restaurants. A theater... an arts theater. I hoped she didn't have that in mind; if so, I'd have a ready excuse, like I couldn't spare the time. I didn't intend to punish myself with some depressing foreign picture, especially so early in the day. No, she probably only wanted to meet me for lunch; no doubt she had some weird, oriental dish in mind, something she could tolerate but would burn my insides out. Maybe even Hindu food with their famous hot curry sauce they say can dissolve your intestines. I wouldn't put any sadistic scheme past her, not after that poolroom date.

My head was spinning. First Cindy to upset me, now Carly to rejuvenate and excite me. I didn't know if I was coming or going. Was my fate in my hands or someone else's? I wished I could be sure. All I knew was that my future was beginning to look extremely interesting.

Grabbing my jacket and snatching my car keys from the sideboard, I headed out of the apartment for my office. I'd already made up my mind: tonight, after work, I'd have dinner at the Four Seasons. Carly probably would be off already, but hopefully I'd get a chance to see Lisa, her roommate. Maybe even talk to her. It wouldn't hurt to have any ally, just in case....

Chapter 9

I saw no blinking light on my answering machine when I came through the door to my apartment. No messages. Good, I thought, stripping off my shirt and tie and moving off to the bathroom where I leaned close to the mirror to give my face a close inspection. I stroked my jaw, grateful for a light beard that didn't need a second shaving in a day. I shaved twice only for the most important occasions. Not a sign of a five o'clock shadow. Not that it made any difference tonight. Carly should be gone. If I could get lucky enough to talk to Lisa, I might pick up some useful hints from her. Getting to know her could be helpful in itself. To do it, though, I'd have to strike up a conversation with her. But would she talk? I was determined to make her like me. Then again, what if she didn't like me? She might rebuff me completely.

I pulled a maroon sweatshirt over my head and combed my hair. I decided not to let her know my real name and play it by ear. Finishing up my ablutions, I threw on an old leather jacket and headed out the door.

It didn't take long to drive to the Four Seasons, fifteen minutes or so. The street and house lights were blinking on already and the workday traffic was still heavy. Darkness was falling dark when I arrived and the glare of headlights hurt my tired eyes. The blast of warm air as I entered the restaurant was a welcome contrast to the cold outside, and the sweet aroma of fresh-brewed coffee sparked my appetite.

The place wasn't very busy. Most of the booths and counter stools were unoccupied. It looked like a clean enough place, and the curtained windows and old-fashioned knotty pine booths lent it a homey atmosphere. I took a stool near the end of the counter and reached for a menu.

"Coffee?" a pert brunette asked, setting down the utensils wrapped in a napkin.

"Sounds good," I said, stealing a quick glance at her ID tag before she turned away. Unless she had changed her name to Irene in the last twenty-four hours, she wasn't Lisa. I scanned the menu, passing up the burgers and settling on the sandwiches.

Irene set my coffee down and whipped out her pad. "Need more time?"

"No, I think I'll have the hot roast beef plate."

"Mashed potatoes, French fries—"

"Mashed, and lots of gravy."

"Peas or carrots?"

"Peas."

"Thank you," she said, briskly moving away.

I stirred a packet of sugar into my coffee, took a sip and casually swiveled on my stool one way and the other to take a better look around. No Carly and no Lisa, not that I could see, anyway. Maybe neither was working. An elderly woman sat alone in a booth, looking forlorn and picking at what looked like a plate of cottage cheese topped with sliced peaches. What stories could she tell? I wondered. Several booths away a middle-aged couple was carrying on an animated conversation I couldn't hear over the piped-in rap music playing a little too loud, a far cry from Sam's Harry James.

Farther down, a few female students with their books piled up on the side occupied a booth. And, almost lost in a booth tucked in a corner by himself sat a disheveled young guy, no doubt from the university, too, writing in a pad and munching on a burger. A few other customers were scattered about, drinking coffee and likely waiting for their orders to be filled.

I swung around as Irene came through the kitchen doors to my right, followed by a redhead carrying an order to a booth near the rear of the restaurant. Irene placed my meal before me.

"Would you like anything else?"

"I'm fine. By the way," I said, offhandedly, "is Carly working tonight?"

"No, I think she went off at three…ready for a warm up?"

"No, not yet, thanks."

"Enjoy."

Peppering my potatoes, I glanced over my shoulder to the waitress coming back.

Without knowing, I knew she was Lisa. I watched her disappear into the kitchen as I cut into my sandwich and took a bite. The meat was tender and the gravy was hot and without the bitter, burnt taste I often got elsewhere.

A few minutes later, the two waitresses emerged from the kitchen.

"It's your section, Lisa." Irene was saying. "Why not?"

"I don't know. I feel…uncomfortable waiting on him."

"He seems nice enough to me, but if you want me to, I don't mind one bit." She laughed a soft, throaty laugh. "I saw him reading a science book yesterday. Maybe he's going to be a doctor and he'll fall in love with me."

Lisa obviously didn't find her amusing. "Sure, lotsa luck."

I quickly averted my eyes as Lisa turned her attention to me. Stepping behind the counter, she picked up a freshly brewed pot of coffee and held it out. "Warm it up for you?"

"Sure," I said, noticing her hand had a slight tremble to it.

I looked at her ID tag, smiled up to her. By then I'd changed my mind and was about to introduce myself when her eyes lit up and she broke into a bright smile of her own. Only she wasn't looking at me; she was focused on the entrance door. I took a quick look over my shoulder and saw a rugged-looking man come in wearing a black leather jacket and brown hat, both of which he took off and hung on a clothes rack off to the side. He gave Lisa a quick nod and slid into a booth close by.

I could sense her excitement as she set the coffee pot back and went quickly around the counter over to his booth where she sat down next to him. The music cut out momentarily and I could hear what they were saying, but only barely.

"David, I didn't expect you tonight. I really didn't. I missed you."

"Baby, it hasn't been that long." He laughed. "But I missed you, too."

His hoarse laugh had a phony ring to my ears. Pretending to look up to the clock on the wall, I stole another quick glance at the guy. He didn't look young, not with those sharp cut lines around his mouth and a head of long, dark hair, styled, like he must have seen in the 1970 television reruns. He had a hard jaw, clean-shaven to blue roots that suggested a hard-boiled personality, a man who looked quick to anger. He might have been old enough to be Lisa's father, but obviously she was hung up on him. I made it a point to ask Carly about him— and her.

Then again, none of this was my business. Who was I to judge anybody else's relationships, especially when I knew nothing of either of them. At one time I would have been quick to give advice, to criticize or condemn and, truth be known, I still had that tendency. I'd been wrong enough times to know it was better to keep my mouth shut and mind my own business. Besides, I had enough trouble trying to understand myself and work out my own problems, especially with Cindy. I could hope she'd give up on me, but I couldn't count on it, not with the Cindy I knew. She didn't get to where she was in business by being soft. From some of the business stories she told me, I knew she was tenacious and when she wanted something, she went after it with a vengeance.

Ignoring Lisa and her friend's conversation and concentrating on the lousy music playing again, I finished my meal and dabbed my mouth with my napkin. Irene had run her order of French fries over to the young customer Lisa wanted no part of and came back.

"Dessert tonight?"

"No, I'll take the bill now."

She tore it off her pad, said, "Thank you," and left.

I picked up the slip, checked the figures, counted out the total and left a five dollar tip.

Lisa was so engrossed in her friend's conversation, she didn't notice me pass her on my way out the door.

Even though I was sure Carly would be off, I was hoping she'd be working. I left disappointed, but the thought of seeing her in a few days gave me a lift. If only it didn't seem like a long time until then. Such a long, long time.

Chapter 10

Tuesday, the day I was to meet Carly, was slow in coming, excruciatingly slow. I busied myself over the weekend poring over briefs that had to be readied for court. It kept my mind occupied, distracted me from thinking of Carly every minute of the day. Even my dreams were disturbed by visions of her. Never had I felt this way toward any girl, especially in so short a time. If it wasn't so exhilarating, it would be scary.

Over and over I relived our moments together, haunted by her beauty, disturbed by her fickle behavior. I analyzed the words I said to her and her responses, trying to discover what triggered the little flash points along the way that had so often disrupted the flow of our conversations and sabotaged the good feelings between us. She had to feel some affection for me, I felt sure. Why else would she want to see me? Why, in fact, did *she* call *me* for a date? I had to laugh. Was it to torment me in some subtle, sadistic way? Judging by the way things were going, I wouldn't put it past her.

She had good reason to be critical of me, though she didn't know it or have any real facts to rely on. As for myself, being an attorney and having to pretend to believe the lies I heard every day in and out of court didn't do much to encourage my faith in mankind. From the littlest guy trying to squeeze a few dishonest bucks out of an insurance company or compensation board, to the pillars of society lying through their pearly teeth trying to gain financial advantage over the investor or their competitors through insider trading or in shady stock and corporate deals— well, I'd seen and heard enough.

And I didn't exclude my own 'honorable' profession. Jokes like: 'You know, it was so cold in New York last week the lawyers had their hands in their own pockets.' Or, 'Business was so bad in the city last year the mafia laid off a dozen judges.' Much truth is to be found in jest, I thought.

I hadn't always been so cynical. Time was when I used to be trusting, too trusting, but I attributed that to youth, to the innocence of youth. Naiveté would be the better word. But being burned by experience took care of that character flaw.

I pondered. Then again, maybe Carly wasn't entirely wrong. Maybe I have gone too far in my distrust of my fellow man, much the way so many police officers regard everyone a potential criminal— guilty till proven innocent. If my thinking was out of balance I'd have to pay more attention to my behavior, my attitude toward others. Something inside resisted, though. It seemed so much safer to trust no one, to take nothing for granted, to keep my guard up. To do otherwise would make me vulnerable. And she, Carly, was proof of that: despite her unpredictability, I trusted her motives to be sincere and her intentions toward me honorable. My instincts had been telling me to break away, to forget her, to spare myself the pain of trusting and believing. So far I'd been successfully ignoring the inner voice that kept whispering to me there's more to this woman than meets the eye. Maybe I was asking for trouble. But no, somehow she'd become too important to me. I made up my mind to trust her and risk the pain that inevitably attaches itself to that questionable virtue. If she offered me an apple, would I, like Adam take it? Samson took a risk, too, and lost. I hoped I wasn't asking for a haircut and heading for the exit gate.

* * * * *

On Tuesday morning I cut my telephone conversations short and hustled to get some of my paperwork out of the way. I told my secretary I'd be gone for a couple of hours, and hurried out of the building down to the parking ramp, where I dropped into the seat behind the wheel of my car and drove out into the busy afternoon downtown traffic.

At 12:00 sharp I swung into the Jamison fire hall lot and was surprised to find it crowded with vehicles, most of them vans, pick-ups and SUVs. Near the end of the building I spotted Carly standing beside her car. She was wearing black slacks and a red waist-length jacket. She stood on her tiptoes and waved me toward an empty space beside her car. I drove up, backed in, climbed out and glanced around, bewildered. Then I understood— of course. This had to be one of those chicken or roast beef barbecues the volunteer firemen or the community often throw to raise money for one charitable cause or another. I smiled inwardly. Good old Carly, always the do-gooder, obviously.

"Are you here to report a fire?" I joked, stunned all over again by a face— even with a minimum of make-up, the blue eyes contrasted with the black hair— a face beautiful beyond recall.

"Not exactly," she said, smiling brightly behind a skein of hair blown suddenly by a gust of wind across her face.

I touched her elbow. "Don't tell me, let me guess: this is one of those charity lunches for the less fortunate."

"No, as a matter of fact—"

"Oh, I get it, it's one of those fund-raising bingo parties. And you feel lucky."

She pointed to the ambulance parked outside the main door. "This is a Red Cross station today, and *we* are going to make a donation."

My blood curdled as the meaning of her words sank in. "A

donation?"

"I've been giving to the blood bank ever since my favorite uncle had his operation six years ago," she said, leading me to the entrance. He needed blood and it was in short supply then, at least his type was. That's when I realized how important it is to give."

Blood bank, hell! Those words were nothing more than a euphemism for a modern house of Dracula. My fear of needles and the sight of blood had kept me from ever giving before, and I didn't know if I could go through with it now, even for her.

"I didn't think you'd mind doing a public service. Unless you're one of those people who are squeamish about such things," she added, in a tone that suggested I might be a coward, a tone very much like the one that had lured me to a near early death at Willy's poolroom.

Surprises were supposed to signal happy events, and having my blood siphoned off was not my idea of a good time. The thought of a needle penetrating my flesh made me woozy. "Squeamish?" I repeated, with a forced hint of derision. "Me?"

"Would you believe there are some people who are actually afraid of a little needle or to give a little blood? Can you imagine such sissies?"

"Only a pint," I croaked, walking on stiff legs and staring zombie-like straight ahead. I could feel my Adam's apple yo-yo-ing in my constricted throat.

"After all," she said, "the human body does contain two gallons of it."

"Oh, really, that much? Well, then, I don't see why anyone should mind, even— the word nearly choked me— sissies." I felt like a sheep being led to the slaughter by a Judas goat.

"You don't have any communicable diseases, do you?" she

teased.

Just this once I wished I could answer in the affirmative.

The door opened and we stood aside to let another couple out. I searched their faces for signs of imminent collapse, but read nothing in their foolish smiles but a bland euphoria one sees on the faces of people leaving Sunday Mass. Or was it the relief one sees in the faces of those who have survived a house fire?

Inside the room—a large, open area—it was hot and stuffy. In the foreground, against the walls and in the center, stood tables and metal chairs set up in stations, with a scattering of donors patiently waiting their turn. The staff bustled about from one place to another, or sat behind tables, riffling through papers and filling out forms. At the far end, half a dozen or so people stretched out on tables, looking eerily like cadavers on morgue slabs. The place had a slight medicinal smell that gagged me.

"Won't you have a seat, sir?"

I eased into the chair a little distance from Carly, who was already seated and giving information to the woman behind the desk opposite her.

"Do you have your donor card, sir?" the woman facing me asked. She had flour-white hair and heavily rouged cheeks.

"I, uh, don't have it with me, no," I stammered, barely able to hear Carly rattle off what sounded like her birth date to the woman checking her answers against her record.

"You have donated before, then, I assume?" she said.

I wondered, could this sweet, innocent-looking, doll-faced woman be part of a conspiracy to hurt me? "A while ago I did," I lied, "quite a while ago. Hard to work these visits into my schedule, you know?" I said, in case Carly could hear me.

"I see. All right, then, let's get some information from you now."

I whispered the answers to the more delicate questions as I peeled off my top coat and folded it over my arm. Finished at last with the lengthy format, I followed the woman's pointing finger to another section where a portly lady with a tooth-friendly grin greeted me warmly:

"And how are *you* this fine day?" she sang out, taking my completed form.

Oh, great, just great. "I'm well, thank you," I answered in a voice too flat to be convincing. Nearby, Carly sat with her legs primly crossed and her elbows in her lap. Her jacket lay on an empty chair behind her. Her eyes squinted a smile at me as a worker pressed a thermometer against her forehead.

Miserable, rankling with the knowledge of having been tricked, I sat stony-faced as my woman did the same thing to me. If ever I prayed for a fever, it was now. She read the number and smiled sweetly. "A perfect 98," she said, handing me a small cup. "Have this juice and take a seat over there, please." She marked my form and gave it to me. Who knew that being perfect could be so depressing.

Numb, feeling detached from reality, I followed her pointing finger around the seats to another row facing the wall, where several small tables crowded with paraphernalia were set up. Each was occupied by a nurse and a donor. I slipped in beside Carly.

"We're lucky," she whispered, checking her watch. "Usually it's so crowded you have to wait."

Whoopee! How lucky can a guy get? I turned away to avoid seeing a man get his ear pierced for a blood sample.

Carly answered the 'next' and took a seat farther down

along the wall.

Getting more depressed by the second, I suddenly felt abandoned, alone, helpless. My emotions see-sawed between anger and despair. And fear, too. The fear that gripped me now was worse than Chief's icy stare and bone crushing handshake; worse even than the prospect of being locked inside the poolroom at the mercy of Hinch and his grungy thugs.

I brooded. I thought of Cindy, good old Cindy. She might be temperamental, hurl ashtrays at me and claw at my face when she was angry, but she never subjected me to anything like this. She wasn't that sadistic. No, and if she were with me now we'd be nestled in some dark little club, cuddling, listening to music, sipping Manhattans (certainly no Bloody Marys). Instead there I was, trapped in this hellish, ghoulish place, a near-paralyzed victim being offered up for sacrifice. I felt as if I were strapped to a conveyor belt, grinding along inexorably, a la the *Pit and the Pendulum,* toward the buzz saw to my doom. And no one to call for help. Somehow I'd lost control and could find no way to reclaim it. The impulse to flee, to escape, was almost overpowering, but at that moment my fear of being shamed in her eyes was even greater than my fear of death.

My eyes glazed over and my clammy hands tugged at my collar, which was beginning to choke me. I was afraid I'd pass out like a coward.

A sudden burst of activity brought my head swiveling around in time to see a number of workers converging on a man pitched head down on a table laid with cookies and snacks. Watching them lift his limp form from the chair and stretch him out on the floor made my hair stand on end. The workers hovered over him like vultures over carrion. They loosened his clothing and whispered commands to each other. Someone shouted for water, another held his arm out while yet another checked his blood pressure. They pumped his legs and called his name, "Mr. Montrose…! Mr. Montrose…!"

After what seemed like hours of a living nightmare, they lugged the man to a cot in the corner and, with a flimsy, portable screen, shielded him from the eyes of the morbidly curious, like me, I'll admit.

My God, was he dead? A quiver of panic shot through me. I'd heard of people dying in exactly this way. I tried not to think of it before, but now how could I avoid it? I couldn't stop the tremble in my hands as I glanced at the people around me, scrutinizing their faces for signs of the same hysteria that was lifting me from my seat.

"Next."

Half-dazed I found myself sitting across from an RN who fired a volley of questions:

"Diabetes?"

"No."

"Heart condition?"

"No."

"Malaria?"

The litany seemed endless. It annoyed me. And unsettled me, too, to think of the vast array of microscopic killers lurking out there to take my life.

"Hepatitis?"

"No."

"Jaundice?"

"No."

I suddenly felt oddly proud of my remarkably good health. To have escaped unscathed the myriad afflictions of life for so many years struck me as nothing short of miraculous. Inwardly, I swelled with a euphoric sense of invincibility.

Efficient, serious, the nurse took my pulse and blood pressure and, at her bidding, I presented my ear. So deftly did she jab my lobe for a blood sample that I hadn't time to jerk away or even wince, as I feared I would.

Well, really, not too bad so far, I thought, if I could only forget Mr. Montrose languishing behind the screen, or maybe even dead. I felt encouraged and not a little ashamed of myself. After all, if all these people— many of them a lot older than I am— if they could do it, if Carly could do it, damn it, so could I!

Pressing a wad of gauze to my ear, I followed this nurse's antiseptic finger, too, to another station. Not seeing Carly ahead, I looked around and spotted her sitting across the room some distance away. She smiled over her fingers waggling 'hi' to me.

I'd hoped we'd be close enough to talk. Disappointed, I proceeded to the assigned table. A matronly woman with powder-blue hair and eyes to match instructed me to fill out a personal form and handed me a plastic bag wrapped with a plastic tube.

"Please fill out the form and deposit the top half in the box there." Smiling, she nodded the direction.

I filled out the form, a final, confidential check of my sex habits, a last-chance-to-fess-up affidavit:

"Have you been with a prostitute within….?"

"Have you been to Zaire within….?"

These volunteers! Their incessant smiles were driving me crazy. So unnatural. So hypocritical. Maybe not actually, but it was certainly all planned and orchestrated, part of their job, to give the whole process the semblance of a happy family gathering. But they couldn't fool me. None of their cheeriness and friendly banter could distract me or make me forget they wanted my blood, literally, that and nothing else. Nor could I forget Mr. Montrose, poor Mr. Montrose, apparently abandoned to his fate and probably assuming room temperature behind the screen.

Wearing a beatific smile, a woman just up from a table passed in front of me, and I couldn't help looking for puncture wounds on her neck.

My mind tilted. Was Carly lying when she said I had two gallons of the red stuff coursing through my veins? If I did, maybe my body needed all of it; if not, why did I have it in the first place? Nature generally knows what it's doing. And was there any guarantee my body could regenerate the loss. Or what if I had an accident on the way home? That pint could make the difference between life and death. I wondered, do these nurses siphon off a little extra to boost their take, the way customers at roadside vegetable stands sometimes slip an extra ear of corn into the bag? I could have a heart attack. I'd heard of such things happening. Or a stroke. My God, just look at Mr. Montrose!

The dread moment arrived, the moment I tried to prepare for, the moment when I feared I'd faint dead away.

Like a marionette suddenly jerked to its feet, I stood woodenly, and woodenly I turned. Across the room I saw Carly's benign and innocent face. Instead of lunging at her and throttling her for putting my life in jeopardy, as my impulses dictated, I returned her smile and, mustering my resolve, launched myself toward the table.

"Your right arm or your left?" the young, strawberry blond asked pleasantly.

"Pardon me?"

"Do you prefer we use your right arm or your left?"

I calculated. My left arm, being closer to my heart, would pump the blood out faster. I'd be finished with the ordeal that much sooner. Then again, if something went wrong, I'd bleed to death faster.

"Better use the right."

"Fine. Roll up your sleeve and lay this way please."

I stretched out on the table, oily smelling and thinly cushioned, and feeling oddly powerless before the slight creature hovering over me.

Again I had to give my name and date of birth. As if anybody would be crazy enough to sub for someone else! I made up my mind: if she asked me for the name of next of kin I'd bolt for the nearest exit. She strapped a flexible band around my upper arm and gave me a hard rubber ball 'to squeeze every five to ten seconds.' Sure, like asking someone to knot the rope you intend to hang him with.

Unable to watch, I stared up to the acoustical ceiling, trying to count the holes in the tiles to keep my mind off the needle I knew she was preparing for me. How thick was that needle, anyway? I remembered hearing jokes about doctors and nurses using square needles. Funny then maybe, not now. And who was the sadist who invented the needle, in the first place? What kind of a mind did it take for someone to say, 'I know, I'll make a real sharp needle with a hole in the end, stick it into a body and suck out the blood.' Even a voodoo witch doctor doesn't do that.

Good grief, what a fool I was to allow myself to get involved in this! I'd rather tangle with a dozen Chiefs at Willy's than submit to this torture and possible death. There at least I'd have a fighting chance. I regretted not making up an excuse as soon as I knew what was happening. I could have feigned pains in my heart or pretended I was having a seizure. Anything. Anything at all to escape this ordeal.

I felt the cool alcohol swab rubbing over my skin, then the dull pressure-pain of the needle puncturing my blood-gorged vein. Now I knew what a helpless fly feels like when a spider sinks its fangs into its flesh. I grew dizzy, light-headed, as though I were falling from a great height. My mind grew dark for an instant, and I thought I'd pass out.

Perhaps sensing my nervousness, the young girl rattled on soothingly of the weather and the 'nice crowd' they were getting as she went about her routine. I heard little of her mindless chatter, and could manage to mumble only incoherent responses. My mind was fixed on the life blood that I knew, but couldn't feel, was exiting my body. Did it drip, I wondered, or did it trickle out? Could it be streaming out? After all, she did tap an artery in my arm; at least I thought it was an artery. If not, it was still a hell of a big vein. 'Save some for the undertaker,' I was tempted to cry out.

After a few moments she left me to myself. Presumably to make my peace with God. I did indeed pray, a very heartfelt prayer, and promised to live a better life if allowed to survive this threat to my existence.

Tilting my head slightly, I could see the legs and torsos of others laid out around me in a manner so resembling a morgue that I wouldn't have been surprised to see bare feet with toe tags dangling from them. An odd sensation passed over me, a vague, self-conscious, voyeuristic feeling I couldn't quite fathom. A sudden erotic impulse tingled me and I closed my eyes against it. In the first place, I didn't want any sinful thoughts in my mind if I was going to see God soon. If it was only some kind of fantasy orgy I was experiencing, it could only be an orgy of death. Maybe that was the subtle, sexual appeal of the Dracula legend.

How could I ever follow in my father's footsteps and become a doctor, when I couldn't even bear to see a needle or a little blood. Worn out with thinking and worrying, I gradually relaxed, resigned to my fate. If my heart failed, so be it. I thought of the five- and ten-gallon donors whose faces I'd seen in the newspaper over the years. They survived, didn't they? Yes, but how many didn't survive that you never hear about? It would be bad publicity for the program, so they'd have to suppress those statistics, wouldn't they? Hopefully, the mortalities really were rare and I'd be one of the many who make it, although possibly I could be the one-in-a-million donor who didn't make it, either. Those odds might seem impossibly long when buying a lottery ticket, but uncomfortably short under the present circumstances.

A drowsiness crept over me. I sank slowly into a twilight doze. But not for long! The piercing thought of succumbing to slow, peaceful death, like that of a carbon monoxide victim, jolted me back to awareness. Alert now, my confidence restored, I returned to squeezing the ball. Doing that made me feel like I was aiding and abetting in my own murder.

How long could I lay here like this, knowing nothing and wondering where the heck Carly was! For all I knew, or anyone knew, the tube could have slipped from the bag under my table and I could be bleeding all over the floor, the way gasoline once spilled over the ground when I carelessly left the pump unattended and overfilled my gas tank. Or what if some maniac or terrorist had crawled underneath my table and intentionally snipped the line. How long would it take to pour out two gallons of blood? Two gallons wasn't all that much.

Time dragged and I grew weary with thinking and worrying. I decided to give up the struggle and let come what will. If this was my karma, so be it. I only hoped Carly was appreciative of the sacrifice I was making for her, a girl I barely knew, had never even kissed, not once, a girl who, from the moment we met, hadn't treated me particularly well, either. I had to be world's number one fool.

I'd also have to watch out for the good deeds I found myself engaging in over the years. I remembered a time not so long ago, when I stopped my car to help a woman who had fallen unconscious on the sidewalk. No sooner had I bent over her, when a cop cruiser screeched up to the curb, doors flying open, and before I could protest or explain, found myself thrown up against a building, frisked and given the third degree. Or the time before that, when I was a much younger Samaritan, reaching into a stranger's parked car to turn off the headlights he had left on. I could still feel the iron grip behind my neck and the near beating I almost got. How true the saying, 'No good deed goes unpunished.'

The thought occurred: Who was getting my blood, anyway? Maybe some undeserving rat. A criminal or even an insurance man, for instance. I'd hate that. Or a used-car salesman. With all the rip-off artists I'd encountered over the years— and their numbers were legion— chances were good that one of them would get it. Even one of those jerks who cut you off in traffic and throw one-finger salutes. The very ones who create the need for blood by causing accidents. And here I lay, sap numero uno, risking my life for the likes of those leeches, those parasites. I bristled.

On the other hand, I could be helping an innocent child or some elderly person who'd given much to the world. Or a destitute mother, a disabled father, a charity worker or a military veteran. Yes, I'd rather believe that. Someone worthy. Surely, there were more than a few of them around. If only I knew for sure. No doubt, Carly would say the good outnumbered the bad. I couldn't go along with her Pollyannaism, but she could be right this time.

"And how are we doing here?" the young girl inquired, appearing above me like a rescuing angel from heaven.

'We' my eye! "Are we done?"

"Yes, we are," she said, beaming and doing whatever she did below my line of sight. She removed the needle, dressed the wound and told me to hold my arm up in the air for a minute.

Waves of relief washed over me. I did it, I actually did it! I made it... so far. I monitored myself for any ill-effects and, surprisingly, detected none. But then, maybe neither did Mr. Montrose at that point.

"Sit up for a minute or two, please," she said, lending a helping hand. "How do you feel now?" she asked.

"Drained."

"Oh, that's cute," she said, steadying me and getting me into position.

My head felt heavy, then light when I swung my legs over the side. I viewed the Band-Aid on my arm as a badge of honor.

When I assured her that I was good, she helped me to my feet and pointed to the exit area. Moments later I was sitting at a table spread with bite-sized ham, and peanut butter and jelly sandwiches, cookies, juice and coffee. The volunteer serving me— another granny-type with a freshly permed head of gray— handed me a Red Cross button to attach to my collar. A Purple Heart, I thought, would be more appropriate.

Glancing around for Carly and breathing a deep sigh, I suddenly remembered that this was the point where Mr. Montrose collapsed. Panicked, I gulped down half my coffee and gobbled up a handful of cookies, as if by so doing I could instantly rebuild my blood supply or blood pressure and forestall a similar fate. A surreptitious glance toward the corner revealed no Mr. Montrose. Gone. By ambulance? Hearse?

Wolfing down more cookies, a plate of minced ham sandwiches and second cup of coffee helped allay my fears.

Walking outside with Carly, I felt immensely proud of myself. "Nothing to it," I boasted, assuming a nonchalant stride on steadier legs than I came in on. "And how about you, Carly? How did you finish up before me? You were still sitting along the side when I was on the table? I hope you didn't pass up the snacks?"

"Oh, it wouldn't be right to take any," she said, "not having given any blood."

"Not—"

"They wouldn't take it." She dug a tissue from her pocket. "The nurse noticed I have a slight case of the sniffles. She said I had a cold and needed the antibodies for myself. I told her I was sure it was just a little allergy that crops up from time to time, but—" She shrugged.

"Too bad, tough break," I said, reeling a little with the revelation.

"I'm really disappointed," she said. "I've never been turned down before."

Oh, that my life should be filled with such disappointments! How ironic to think she, altruist, goodwill ambassador to the world, had sat comfortably aside, while I, skeptic and cynic, had suffered for someone I'd never know. It didn't help diminish my belief that life was eminently unfair. In fact, it reinforced it.

Still…she had wanted to give. Her heart was in the right place, and that's what really counted. And Mr. Montrose, no one forced him there, and he'd probably be back despite his reaction, if he was still alive, that is. To say nothing of those multiple-gallon donors. I felt a twinge of shame.

I rebuked myself for behaving like a juvenile, for making a

sham out of something noble and good, for feeling resentment toward all those who gave their time or their blood or both for a worthy cause. And I had to admit to myself, I really felt good down deep inside, knowing I might be helping to save a life? Not to mention the victory I'd won over myself. No small accomplishment, that. Would I do it again? Well, if Carly asked, probably... but darn, if only I hadn't seen that poor Mr. Montrose...! I'd like to think I would, but I wasn't sure I'd come quite that far, not yet anyway. As the saying goes, 'baby steps first!'

"Sooo...." She drawled as we reached her car.

"How about some lunch?"

She laughed. "You mean you're still hungry? After eating in there like you were going to the electric chair?"

"I have a big appetite. We could go to Sam's, it's not far from here, listen to Harry James."

"It sounds inviting, Bryan, it honestly does, but between my classes and work, I don't have a minute to spare. I had to squeeze the time out to come here this afternoon."

"Can't you squeeze out another hour?"

"Can you call me tomorrow?" she said, seeing the obvious pain in my eyes. "It'll give me a chance to get organized and sort things out."

"Coffee, at least?"

"Honest, I can't, Bryan, much as I'd love to." She opened her car door, swept her pants smooth beneath her and slid in. "Thanks for coming. It meant a lot to me." She reached out and touched my hand. "You know, Bryan, for a while there, I thought you looked nervous and were afraid to give blood."

"Me? Are you kidding? I'd have given a quart if they

wanted it. Two quarts."

"I'm glad I was wrong," she said, smiling in a way I knew she didn't really believe me.

"Okay, then," I said, slapping the hood, "I'll call you tomorrow."

Crestfallen, I watched her drive off, hearing her coughing muffler fade in the distance. 'Call tomorrow,' she said. Tomorrow. I hated the word. It meant promise without guarantee, hope without substance. I could be dead tomorrow!

I stalked back to my car feeling like Casey at the Bat, the last of the Mohicans, Robinson Crusoe, odd man out. Why is it, I wondered, that women, even when they care for a man, can be as secretive as a sphinx and patient as a cat stalking prey, while men like me are forever kids on the night before Christmas: anxious, jumpy, impatient? God must have been feeling diabolical when he created woman. Even more so when he created this one.

Chapter 11

All the following day I had a difficult time concentrating on my work. I was still feeling the stress that began the moment I stepped into the fire station and realized it was being used as a blood bank. Inwardly I felt ticked over Carly playing such a dirty trick on me. Of course she couldn't know how much I hated seeing blood and needles, but she should've known I could have been one of those squeamish people. She put me at risk of humiliating myself. Fortunately, I managed to put on a pretty good act, at least I thought I did.

Despite everything, it perplexed me no end wondering why I couldn't get Carly off my mind, even for fifteen minutes. Sure, she was beautiful, especially when she fixed me with those devastating blue eyes; sure she had a charming and winning way about her, even when she was being difficult or even downright hostile. Something about her made me weak in the knees when I was in her presence, soft in the head, too, in a manner of speaking— or maybe not in a manner of speaking.

My intercom buzzed. "Yes?"

"CEO Franklin Stepp from Lyford Industries is on the phone. He'd like to speak to you about the papers you've been working on."

I looked at my watch: 3:55. "Tell him I'm in a meeting and I'll get back to him by 10:00 tomorrow morning."

'Tell him I'm in a meeting' is probably as common an excuse in the business world as is 'The check is in the mail' to the general public. And just as transparent, I thought, scooping up a handful of documents and slipping them into a manila folder. I never liked to put people off like that. I didn't like it when it was done to me, and it had been, as with everybody else, countless times, but I knew Stepp was a talker who'd keep me on the phone for an hour.

Setting a fat file next to a leaning stack of equally fat files, I made ready to leave for the day. Earlier, I picked up the phone to call Carly, but changed my mind. I didn't want to appear too eager, even though I could have covered myself by saying I wasn't sure what time of the day was best for her, with her obligations and all. Of course I was certain I wouldn't be fooling her one bit. In the end I decided it best to wait until evening.

Again the intercom: "Mr. Perri, your mother's on the line."

"Mom."

"Bryan, are you busy?"

"I'm just getting ready to leave."

"Did you make plans for supper tonight?"

"Not yet, why?"

"I have lots of turkey left over from Sunday because you couldn't make it. Even the chocolate cake I baked for little Davey's birthday is left over."

"You mean my brother didn't gobble the whole thing down himself?"

"He tried to, believe me, but I told him, 'Tom,' I said, 'you save some for Bryan, he likes it too, you know.' He said, 'Too bad for you.' I think he was put out because you didn't come for Davey. Anyway, I said, 'Too bad, nothing,' and took it away. Like I said, Bryan, there's lots left over. I can't eat it all myself and it would be a sin to throw it all away. So, do you want to stop over for supper tonight?"

I hesitated, considering the possibility of seeing Carly later that evening, then gave the thought up as wishful thinking. "Sure, Mom. I'll be over in half an hour or so."

* * * * *

Minutes later I cruised the boulevard across town to the neighborhood where I was born and raised and where my mother still lived by herself. Gauging my speed, I tried to time the traffic signals along the way. Even though I knew it never saved me more than a few minutes driving time, I always felt I scored a victory against adversity whenever I made a light and didn't have to stop and wait for it to change. If I had one wish in life, I thought, I'd want an automatic signal changer, a little gizmo with a button that I could press and turn the signal green whenever I approached an intersection. To never have to stop again. What a dream! What a lifelong convenience it would be. How much time I could save! I could more than make up the time I lose shaving every day.

Twenty-five minutes later I wound my way through the staid, residential area, wheeled around a final corner, and pulled up in front of the house, a modest ranch, which, like the other houses on the street, was cloistered among shrubbery, evergreens and a variety of maple trees, nearly denuded now.

"Hi, Mom," I called, tossing my coat and suit jacket over a chair near the door. "Smells good."

"It's almost ready," she called back from the kitchen. "I hope you're good and hungry."

"Hungry enough," I said, turning on the television.

My mom came to the kitchen doorway stirring a bowl she held against her bosom. "Bryan, can't you ever leave that thing off when you come in the house? Come in here and sit and talk to me while I warm up the potatoes."

I clicked off the set. "I like to keep up with the events of the day," I said, pulling up a kitchen chair and sitting down. "You never know, they might be looking for me."

She smiled. "You're just like your father, the way I knew him when we first started going together." She removed a bowl of corn from the microwave oven and set it smoking on the table. Slipping the oven mitt from her hand she stood looking down at me. "Are you feeling all right?" she asked, frowning. "You look a little drawn. Are you getting enough sleep?"

"I'm fine," I said, setting up the utensils in front of me. "I guess I've been working a little too many hours lately."

She studied me with her motherly probing eyes. Then you better let up and take it easy before you get run down and sick." She turned away to lift a pot from the stove. "I hope you're eating right. You have to keep your strength up or you'll end up in the hospital like Mrs. Masterson's son, Bill. Poor boy," she said, setting a plate of turkey parts on the table, "working himself half to death in that construction business."

"Nothing's easy, Mom. It's the price you pay when you go into business for yourself—long hours." I jabbed my fork into a turkey thigh.

"It doesn't have to be that way, not to my thinking. You have to be sensible. If Bill had a wife to watch after him...."

Here it comes, I thought. She always finds a way to bring up the subject of marriage. Never fails. It was why I didn't come over to visit as often as I might. And it was worse when my brother Tom and his wife were there; then they'd really gang up on me. I scooped a mound of mashed potatoes onto my plate and ladled on the hot gravy, so much tastier than the gravy I had on my roast beef at the Four Seasons where Carly worked. Nobody in the world could cook like my mother.

"It's not healthy living alone," she said. "It's not natural, Bryan. Your father used to say that, and he was a doctor. He knew." She set out the rest of the dishes and sat down across the table from me.

"Things are a little different today, Mom," I said, filling up the rest of my dish with stuffing, corn and squash. I poured myself a glass of milk from the jug on the table.

"Why do people always say that, as if today makes things better than yesterday? Your father used to say if something works, leave it alone. He said when people change things that work, they usually end up with a lot worse than they had before. It's a step backward, not forward."

I watched her as she spoke, still a sprightly, animated lady whose smooth skin and lively eyes belied her fifty-something years. Coloring her hair dark made her look even more youthful.

"Dad had a point."

"Dad was wise, very wise." I could feel her watching me as she sipped her coffee. "Bryan... have you found a nice girl yet? You know your father was twenty-six when he married me, almost two years younger than you are now."

As expected, she finally came out with it. "Mom, I know you're afraid I'm going to be left out in the cold with no one to look after me, but believe me, I'm all right."

"Yes, now you are. But down the road. It comes fast. Time—"

"Actually, Mom, I did meet a girl I like quite a bit, but I don't know her very well yet, so I can't promise anything."

"How old is she?"

I salted my corn. "About my age, maybe a few years

younger."

"Living alone like you are—don't use so much salt—living alone is not good. At least for now while you're single you should be here in this house. In your own room, instead of letting it go to waste like it is. And why should you spend all that extra money for an apartment downtown when you don't have to, when everything here is free. Your clothes are washed, a clean bed, a hot meal on the table when you come home from work..."

"It's tempting, Mom, but where I'm at is much easier for me. I don't have to fight all the traffic the way I would here, especially in the winter. I know it costs—"

"What does she do, this girl you met? What's her name?"

"Carly Miller. She's a waitress."

"A waitress? And you're a lawyer. You'd be a good catch for her."

"She's a waitress part-time. Actually, she goes to the university. She's taking post grad courses because she wants to teach. She's not quite there yet, though."

"A teacher. Well, that's nice, very nice, especially for a girl. She would make a good wife for a lawyer. And she's a good age."

I laughed. "She doesn't know I'm a lawyer. I told her I was an insurance investigator."

She folded her arms and nodded. "So you'd be sure she wasn't interested in your money. Or the money she would think you make."

"Not really, Mom," I said, cleaning up the last of my potatoes. "I think I wanted to avoid the kind of questions I always get whenever I date a girl. You know, 'Do you defend murderers and rapists?' Or 'Why don't lawyers use simple language everybody can understand?' Or 'What is—'"

She jumped up suddenly. "Oh, my, I forgot the cranberry sauce! Your father wouldn't eat turkey without it." She brought the bowl over and set it in front of me. "So you like this girl, Carly. You like her a lot?" she asked, sitting down again.

"Mom, I hate to say, because if nothing develops I know you'll be disappointed. You want me married and settled like Tom. And have a bunch of little Daveys."

"There's nothing wrong with that."

"I know it. It's just that I'm not rushing into anything until I'm pretty darned sure it's the real thing."

Unconsciously, she twisted the wedding band on her finger. "You know, I was never educated like your father. I never went past high school."

"Dad was a doctor, but what—"

"Just because she's a waitress and probably comes from a poor family doesn't mean she's low class or can't be a good wife. Besides, once she gets her education, who'll care. The most important thing is that you love her and you're sure she loves you. Nothing else matters. Some people may talk, try to give her the impression she's not good enough for you, especially as you get up in the world, maybe be a judge someday— that can be hard. Your father, though, he always stood by me. Maybe it hurt our social life a little but it didn't concern him. He wasn't the snooty type who needed important friends, a mansion and a Cadillac. He never let those rumors get me down. Oh, there were rumors all right, some I'm too ashamed to mention but he was strong for me. And I never made him sorry he stuck by me."

Finished, I put my fork down and sat back in my chair. "I'm

the one who made him sorry."

"Oh, Bryan, it isn't true. Yes, he was disappointed. From the time you were a little boy, his heart was set on your going to medical school and follow in his footsteps because he knew you had the brains to be a doctor. You could have gone into practice with him. I know he looked forward to it."

"But I didn't want it, Mom. I hated hospitals from the day he first took me to visit one he worked in, hated them then and hate them now. And needles and bandages and blood, I hate them, too, and even the color white and the pictures of lungs and colons and hearts they tape to the walls in the examination rooms. I hate it all, right down to the antiseptic smell of a doctor's office." I was glad I wore a long-sleeve shirt so I wouldn't have to explain the bandage I still had on my arm.

"You don't have to convince me, Bryan," she said, her face elongated with sadness. "I understand. You take after me. I couldn't be a nurse if I tried, but you're even worse. I just wish he'd have lived longer. In time he'd have understood, especially seeing how you're already getting a good reputation in the city like you are, and to be so young. I know he'd be very proud of you. I want you to believe me, Bryan."

"If you say so, Mom."

"Yes, I do say so!"

I smiled across to her. She had a sweetness and an intelligence and a down-to-earth-ness that all the college studies in the world couldn't improve upon. His father was indeed a lucky man. And he was lucky to have her for a mother. If Carly turned out to be half the woman—

"Was it good?"

"Delicious."

"Good. Do you want some coffee? It's still warm. And some

of little Davey's birthday cake?"

"Can't pass that up, sure."

"You look just like your father, sitting there with your leg crossed over," she said, filling my cup…. "Why are you looking at your watch? Do you have somewhere to go?"

"No, Mom, I just have to make a phone call."

"To her?" Her eyes twinkled knowingly.

"I've never been able to fool you."

"You can call from here." She smiled. "I won't listen, I promise."

"It's okay, Mom. I don't think she's home yet, anyway. I'll call from my apartment." I cut into the cake. "So what's the latest with Aunt…."

* * * * *

Back in my own apartment, I flopped in my recliner, snatched up my cell phone and tapped in the numbers for Carly's and Lisa's landline phone.

"Hello."

"Carly?"

"No, this is Lisa."

"Hi, Lisa, this is Bryan Perri. Is Carly home or—"

"Hold on, she's right here."

A little abrupt, I thought.

"Hello, Bryan."

"I hope I'm not calling too late?"

"No, it's not even 9:30. I just walked in the door about ten minutes ago."

"Well, I'm not going to keep you. You must be pretty worn out."

"I'm not exactly a bundle of energy, but I'm all right. And I still have homework to do."

"Do you think we could get together, say, Friday evening? I can get tickets to—"

"Friday I can't, Bryan. I'd love to get out, but I'm loaded with work."

I felt let down. "How about the weekend? It'll do you good to get away from all the pressures for a while. To be perfectly frank, I could use a little escape myself." I tried to hide the plaintiveness in my voice.

"I know it's hard to believe, Bryan, but between school and my job and a laundry list of chores, honest, I'm just buried under a ton of stuff to do."

I thought I heard Lisa in the background say, 'Give the guy a break.'

I was about to tell her that if she wasn't interested or if there was someone else in the picture, she could come right out and tell me, when she interrupted my thought with, "Bryan, what if I see you for a couple of hours on Saturday afternoon. Would that be all right?"

"Saturday?"

"Yes, about three o'clock? I'll make sure I work the time into my schedule."

'Oh, great, thanks,' I wanted to say, 'how generous.' Did it ever occur to her that I might have a schedule of my own? "Okay, fine with me. Any ideas how you want to spend the time?" I was tempted to add, 'Do you think you can spare a whole two hours?'

"Why don't we go to that nice little Italian restaurant?"

"Sam's. Great idea. Will you want to eat there?"

"No, only for coffee. Three is too late for lunch and too early for dinner."

She said 'dinner.' That's what my mother used to say the 'snooty' people called it. To my family it was supper. "Good enough. Do you want me to pick you up at your place?"

"Why don't we just meet there? It will save time and make it a little easier all around."

We spoke a few minutes longer before hanging up.

Saturday, 3 o'clock. Sam's. An excellent idea. I hoped it would establish some kind of a mutual tie: the place where we first met—well, almost the first— where we first heard some of Sam's old music. Some of it was catchy, I had to admit, more than catchy—downright pretty after listening awhile, especially that song, 'You Made Me Want You,' or whatever Sam called it. It would forge a kind of bond between us, create an atmosphere of sweet nostalgia we'd always remember as ours, ours alone, and begin a tradition of sorts. Already I'd come to associate the song with her. Sometimes I even caught myself humming the tune, when I could remember it, which wasn't always the case. Of course, that didn't mean she felt the same. Then again, she was the one who suggested the restaurant. If I meant anything at all to her, she would surely always remember Sam's as the place where we first looked into each other's eyes and tried to understand each other's mind. If she forgot the subtle hostilities that had occasionally arisen between them, all the better.

All that thinking was wearing me out. I grabbed the remote, turned on the television, loosened my tie, pushed my recliner back into a near-prone position and within minutes dropped in a light sleep. Suddenly my eyes popped open, prompted by a single, terrible thought: What if this was another one of her rotten tricks!

Chapter 12

Finding Carly's car empty in Sam's parking lot, I checked my watch, took one last peek through her windshield and strode into the restaurant. It took a moment for my eyes to adjust to the semi-darkness, then I spotted her in the same booth we occupied the first time we were there together. The sweet smell of warm bread and spicy sauce hit me pleasantly as I made my way over to her.

"Hi," I said, stripping off my leather jacket and laying it on the seat. "Waiting long?"

She appraised me with a cool smile I didn't quite know how to take. "Only a few minutes," she said. Her hair flowed shiny black over her shoulders to the front of a pale- green turtleneck sweater. The gold pin over her breast matched the small gold buttons hugging her earlobes.

Sam swept up beside us just as I sat down. "Back again, I see," he said, smiling broadly. "I thought maybe you forgot."

"We couldn't do that," I said, "could we, Carly?"

She smiled up to him. "Never. Bryan and I had too good a time the last time we were here."

"Carly. Carly...Miller. Am I right?" Sam said proudly. "Like Carly Simon and Glen Miller. And Perry... Bryan Perry. That name Perry I can't forget, either. Like Perry Como, only 'at'sa his first name. He's dead now, too. The good ones, they're all dead."

I let him believe the spelling of my last name was the same.

"I'm really flattered you remembered our names," Carly said.

"Usually, names I'm not so good on, but faces, them I never forget." He smiled even more broadly. "Especially the beautiful ones," he said, looking directly at Carly

I saw her blush as she quickly arranged the napkin on her lap. "Thank you, Sam, but you're just being kind."

He laughed. "You don't believe me? Take a look at him, how he looks at you."

Now it was my turn to blush.

"So," Sam asked, rubbing his hands together. "Do you want to order something to eat? Something to drink?"

"Nothing to eat today, Sam," I piped up, "unless you want something, Carly."

"No, I'll just have coffee, if it's made, or a soft drink—"

"For you I make the coffee fresh. No problem."

"Same for me, Sam. But we'll be getting here for one of your good meals soon. It's a promise."

Sam held his hands up, like a cop stopping traffic. "I understand. You young people, always so busy these days. No problem. You stay and sit as long as you want. It's okay. We get busy later, not now, so no problem. Even if we are busy, still no problem." He turned to go. "I put some nice music on for you, too. Romantic."

"I'm glad to see you," I said, dazzled by her radiant smile. "I didn't think we were ever going to get together again."

She lowered her eyes. "Everything's been so overwhelming. These teachers think they're the only one you have and they just pile on the work."

This was the opening I was hoping for. I was still feeling out of sorts ever since we parted several days earlier. I know it was because of the way she tricked me into giving blood. I was feeling perverse and couldn't stop myself. "You said you want to teach."

"Yes, Special Education. I think there's a great need for teachers in that field."

"So I've heard. Why is that?"

She shrugged. "I suppose because we have so many more kids nowadays."

"Wasn't there a need for specialized teachers before?"

She paused to think. "Yes, I suppose so."

"Well, what did the schools do before they had them? And before they had these Special Education classes they're writing about these days?"

"I don't know. I suppose they were mixed in with the regular kids." She studied me narrowly. "Don't you believe in the program?"

"Heck, I don't know anything about it except what I read in the newspapers every time they want to increase the school budget and, of course, what I pick up here and there." Actually, I actually l heard a couple of teachers arguing the very same subject at a table next to me in a downtown cafeteria only a week ago. "The reason I'm asking you is because you're on the inside track and have more knowledge than I do."

"Well, a lot of children are getting the specialized help they need and wouldn't otherwise have. They'd be left behind."

"Sounds like a noble endeavor."

Soft music started up in the background, with a pleasing voice singing.

"It's giving children a chance to make it in the world," she said. "They need personalized attention to help overcome their problems. You know, the usual ones we hear about every day, the broken homes, drugs, child abuse and all that."

I nodded understanding. "And what about these new words they keep coming up with, like 'mainstreaming.' What's that all about?"

"It simply means putting these slow or disturbed children into regular classes with average students. One of the reasons is so they don't feel different or like social outcasts. It's a matter of protecting their self-esteem. Another reason is they might benefit intellectually from a more normal environment."

Puzzled, I looked at her. "Isn't that where they were to begin with? Before they moved them out because of their so-called learning problems?"

"Their disabilities, yes, which come in all varieties, of course. But—"

"So now they're putting those same students back where they couldn't hack it in the first place."

Her eyes flashed. "I don't believe you're getting the picture."

"Well, let me try to get it in focus: First they took the slow or troubled kids out of regular classes because they couldn't make it there, and they put them in Special Ed classes with a new class of specialized teachers so that they can get the personal attention they need. Now they've decided it's best to put these same kids back in the regular classes and call it 'mainstreaming.' The schools are spending a lot of extra taxpayer money to do what didn't cost a penny before, only now it has a fancy name. Am I missing something here?"

"Not all of them are put back, only those who have improved enough to warrant it."

"Oh, I see. Well, I won't ask for percentages. Anyway, how about that other new label I've been hearing more and more about? ODD, I think they call the condition."

She appraised me coolly. 'Oppositional Defiance Disorder.' What of it?"

"Where did this so-called disorder suddenly come from? And who discovered it? I mean, is it a genetic disease or a viral or bacterial affliction of the brain or nervous system or what?"

"It's a specific learning disability that certain children have." She bristled. "But I think you already know what it is, so do you mind telling me where this is going?"

"You want an honest answer?"

She sat back folding her arms. "No. Why don't we change the subject and talk about something else."

I had obviously pushed her too far. "Sorry, Carly, I didn't mean to upset or offend you, but—"

"You didn't. I don't feel I need to defend myself or any of the programs I'm involved with."

"Carly, that wasn't my intent. I only—"

"Of course it was, so let's drop the subject, shall we?"

"All right, Carly, all right, it's dropped."

We sat quietly, saying nothing. She couldn't know it, of course, but I had planned this little sneak attack, although I never guessed it would become so intense. I felt she was hiding not only from me but from herself, as well. I wanted to make her uncomfortable, not angry. I wanted to rile up a little, get her to let her guard down and maybe reveal more about herself. I could see now I wasn't merely probing, I was irritating and obnoxious to the point of losing her. If those daggers shooting from her eyes meant anything, I was certain I'd already sealed my own fate. Finally I spoke up:

"I'm sorry, Carly. I have no excuse for acting like a jerk, but will you let me ask you what I really want to know? A personal question?"

She flounced in her seat, her piercing, blue eyes fixed on me. "I'm not sure I want to hear this or whether I'll give you an answer, but go ahead," she said, her voice as tight as a cap on a charge of dynamite.

"Are you in a relationship?"

"What kind of relationship?"

"I mean, is there anyone in your life you're involved with? Romantically?"

"Is there anyone in your life you're involved with? Romantically?"

"No."

A little smile lifted the corner of her mouth. "Not even the mysterious caller you mistook me for?"

"Oh, her. No, Carly, that's over. It's been over for a while."

"It sounded very much like an ongoing relationship."

"Believe me, Carly, it's over, done, dead."

"Are you sure, Bryan?"

"I really am, Carly," I said, starting to sweat a little. "I really am."

She broke out into a full smile. "I'm sorry, Bryan, I have no excuse for acting like a jerk," she said, mimicking me.

I sank back in my chair. "Touche, Carly, touché."

"What's good for the goose...," she said, her expression as icy as the tone of her voice. "For a while there I thought I was in a court of law."

It was time to come clean with her and let her know I was a lawyer. "As a matter of fact, Carly—"

Just then Sam appeared, bearing the serving tray like a libation. Momentarily perplexed by the obvious tension between us, Sam paused and glanced warily at our faces before setting the cups down. "This song, you hear it?" He cupped his hand over his ear. "Frank Sinatra, with his first voice. *All or Nothing at All.* Afterwards when he's older it's different, his voice is deeper and more mellow. The words, listen, you'll love it, I promise, if you never heard it before. He's another one gone now." He sighed. "Too bad we can't live forever, eh? The great ones, anyway. Ah, what can you do?"

Sam faded away and we turned our attention back to ourselves.

"I don't know if it's such a good idea to live forever," I said, picking up on Sam's comment, and grateful for the diversion. "What do you think?"

Her eyes fixed on me as she lifted her coffee cup to her lips and said, "Why are you doing this to me?"

The chill in her voice chilled me and I pretended not to understand. "Doing what?"

"You're trying to upset me and I'd like to know why."

"I didn't mean to if I did," I said, leaning back, as if trying to dodge a bullet.

"You're making me defend myself against… against your arguments."

"You mean against my cynicism?"

"So I'm right, it's not my imagination, you have been goading me."

I sat forward again, desperately wanting to reach across the table and take her hand to reassure her of my affection and sincerity, but I dared not chance rejection. "Carly, if I'm honest with you, promise me you won't get up and scoot out of here, at least until I've finished. Promise?"

"I'm listening."

"Promise?"

The word refused to pass her lips. "I won't leave until you're finished."

"All right, here's what I think, and you can take it or leave it, agree or disagree with me. All I ask is that you try not to take it personally... Whenever anyone sees the world through the proverbial rose-colored glasses, I become— well, I hate to use the word 'suspicious'— but I do become dubious of that person's version of whatever his or her story is, especially where my welfare is concerned. I'll go further— and I don't mean that this necessarily applies to you— but I even become skeptical of their judgment."

Her nostrils flared as she deliberately set her cup back on the saucer, all of which scared the daylights out of me.

"I'm not saying there's anything wrong with being optimistic," I hurried on. "Actually that's good, it's a positive thing, but idealism is something else altogether. When it's not tempered by reason or just plain common sense it becomes risky business and can lead to only God knows where. If you pay attention to the kind of trouble this country has gotten— but that's neither here nor there. What I'm really talking about is balancing idealism with reality. And reality, however unpleasant, can't simply be ignored because we don't like it or don't want to face it. Ugly, cruel things do exist in our world. In our personal lives."

"You're thinking of that poolroom, of my attitude before we

went there."

"No, I wasn't, but now that you bring it up, that experience is a good example of what I'm trying to say."

Her expression changed from a subtle hostility to an amused tolerance. "You wouldn't want to examine the other side of that coin, would you?"

"We're only talking, making friendly conversation," I said, trying to make light of a situation that had become far more serious than I had intended it to be. "I don't mind at all."

"You seem to think that I can only see the bright side—"

"No, no, I meant—"

"Let me finish. If everyone saw only the negative side of things, would we have ever progressed beyond being hunter-gatherers? Would we even have had fire?"

"So," I said, "we're back to cynicism versus idealism."

"I don't know if that's really what we're talking about at all. And I wonder if you do?"

Oh, yes, I certainly did, and it had nothing to do with Special Education, except perhaps as it concerned her choice of vocation. It had everything to do with her presenting herself to the world in one kind of light while she really existed in shadows I couldn't yet penetrate. I'd been seeing the ideal Carly, but was she the real Carly? It would take time, I knew, and now was not the time. I decided to end the 'inquisition,' as she had called it. Already I'd dug a grave deep enough to bury myself in standing up.

"You're right. I guess I get carried away sometimes, I admit it, but only for the sake of livening up the party, so to speak. For a minute there even I thought I was on a soap box. Bygones?" I said, saluting her with my cup.

"I hope you're simply not being condescending," she said, "because I've just begun to fight." She returned my salute with her cup and a smirk.

God, I loved looking at her, even with blue flames dancing in her eyes.

"Hey, folks," Sam called from the back. "More coffee?"

"Please, when you get time," Carly answered.

"Coming right up." He said something to his wife, then, "Carly, tell me if you like this one":

Let's fall in love,

Why shouldn't we fall in love?

Our hearts are made of it,

Let's take a chance,

Why be afraid of it?...

"It is pretty," she said to Bryan, "don't you think so?"

"I really like it. I think that's Sinatra, too," I said smiling, "but I'm not sure if it's his first or second voice."

Sam appeared with his coffee pot and refilled our cups. "You like the music?" he asked, setting the cream aside and looking from her face to mine.

"We were just commenting on it," Carly said. "It's really pretty."

"Thank you, I think so, too. Can I get you something, a little something, anything?"

"No, thank you, Sam," she said, "we'll be leaving shortly."

He shrugged. "If you change your mind, call. I'm helping Caterina in the back. Pretty soon now, we get busy."

"I wonder if everyone gets like that when they get old?" she said. "Living in the past."

"I suppose it's natural. The past always seems better because we tend to forget the bad things that happened. We develop selective memory. The present's too fresh for that."

She frowned. "Not always. The past can be horrible for some people."

"You're probably right. But for Sam you have to consider, too, that he's no doubt seen more happiness than he's likely to ever see in the limited time he has left."

She nodded. "He's apparently happy, but somehow it all seems so sad." She blew on her coffee before taking a sip.

"I suppose life is sad. Like Sam said, it's too bad we can't live forever."

"Would you want to, really, to live forever?"

I wanted to say I would if I could be with her forever. "I suppose not, at least not in the kind of world we know today. Too much grief." I chuckled. "Of course, if someone came up to me every day and asked if I want to die at that moment or tomorrow, I'd opt for tomorrow. I could conceivably live a million years that way."

"It's always easier to say we'll do something than to actually do it."

"How about reincarnation?" I asked. "Would you like that?"

"No, thank you. I can't imagine going through life again in another body."

"If you could live your life over, would you do it

147

differently?"

Trouble lines crossed her forehead. "Would you?"

"If I did, I wouldn't wait to meet up with you in a cemetery. I'd look you up a lot sooner. Someplace more... more alive."

"This silly idealist? Why would you want to do that?"

"Let's not use that word anymore. Let's compromise and say you're a romanticist. You like people, you trust people, you see the best in everyone and everything. Beautiful music moves you. When the last song was playing, I could see it in your face, your expression. It was... wistful...and maybe something more I couldn't read in it." I wondered if she heard the words in her head the way I did: *Let's take a chance, why be afraid of it?*

A party of four—two couples—came in through the door laughing, and took a table across the room. Sam's head peered through the pass-through window. "Be right with you folks."

I leaned across to her. "Carly, if I'm going too far, stop me. I don't mean to pry, but sometimes you seem so distant, and other times—forgive me if I'm wrong—but you seem hostile toward me for no apparent reason. Of course, today I gave you a reason, but that was dumb of me. What I'm trying to say is that I can't be sure if you like me at all, or whether you're tolerating me out of courtesy... Carly, if something's troubling you or you have someone else on your mind... what I mean is, if you care for—"

She slid her hand across the table and laid it on mine. "Oh, no, don't say that, Bryan. There's nobody else, really. In fact, I don't date much at all."

"Working and school—"

"Not only that," she said. "I just haven't been interested in having a relationship. I didn't want to be..."

"Hurt?" I finished for her.

"I was going to say 'obligated.'" She gave my hand a slight squeeze. "And I do like you, Bryan, an awful lot. But I don't think it's fair to you to have to put up with me and my job and my school and everything else. I know you probably think I've been putting you off on purpose, but, honestly, you're the first guy I've enjoyed myself with in... in a long time."

If hearts could sing, mine would have performed an aria. "Believe me, I don't mind at all, I understand, I really do. As long as I know you want to get together whenever it's possible, I'm okay with it."

"There's that song again," she said, her hand still on mine.

"You Made Me Want You," I said.

"You Made Me Love You," she corrected.

I wrapped my hand around hers and held it firmly. "Carly..." I wanted to say something, but didn't know exactly what. I knew only that my chest felt hollow and my breath was coming short. "Carly, I really like being with you," I said. "Don't think I'm going off the deep end here or getting too serious, but I can't remember when I last felt so good doing—doing nothing."

She laughed softly. "Well, I like that. Being with me is 'doing nothing'?"

I knew she was teasing me, that she understood, but I couldn't smile. "You know what I mean."

"Yes, of course I know what you mean," she said in apologetic tone of voice.

"I'm comfortable with you. More than comfortable. I feel like I've known you all my life. As if I've known you in a former life." I could hardly speak, seeing her eyes, moist and warm, gazing across to me. "At the same time you're like no one I've ever met before. It sounds crazy, I know, but it's true."

She drew her hand away from mine and lowered her eyes. "I think it's too soon to—"

"No, I'm not trying to—I mean, I'm just saying that I like being with you and hope you—"

"I appreciate your feelings, Bryan, I really do. I find your company very enjoyable..." her eyes flashed "...even when we're on opposite sides of an argument."

My emotions were running rampant and I fought to keep them under control. She already said she enjoyed my company and wanted to see me again. That was progress. No sense pushing. To press her further would only hurt my cause. I tried to smile.

The song was just ending. "That melody is haunting," I said.

She arched her brow. "Oh, so you were listening to the music and not to me?"

"Actually, I couldn't distinguish between your voice and the music."

Her laugh came soft and bubbly. "Now that is really stretching it."

I laughed with her. "You do have a sweet voice, though. I really mean it."

"Well that's a first, being complimented on my voice."

We drank our coffee and made small talk for a while and listened to Sam's records playing. At last she glanced at her watch. "I think I should be going now."

"Already? Are you sure you don't want to have something to eat? You must be getting hungry."

"Next time, all right?" she said, smiling across to me. She stood up to put on her jacket and I slipped out of my seat to help her.

"Business is starting to pick up. That's nice to see." I looked around but Sam was nowhere in sight. I put on my jacket. "Sam must be busy in the back." I pulled out a ten dollar bill and tucked it under the saucer. "Shall we?" I said, indicating the way out.

Fading rapidly outside, the hard autumn light hurt my eyes. The smell of burning leaves tinged the frosty air. Taking Carly's arm I guided her down the several steps to the parking lot and walked her toward her car.

"Chilly, isn't it?" she said, giving a little shiver with her shoulders.

I hated leaving her so soon. Not knowing when I'd see her again or for how long bothered me. Busy as she was—

A misstep or a hole in the ground— whatever it was— she suddenly tripped, pitched forward, and was on her way down when my grip tightened on her arm and scooped her back up into my other arm, encircling her waist and pulling her in close. I could feel the heat from her face, her warm breath, inches from my own. For a long moment our eyes locked, as if reading each other's very souls, while something electrical, something magical passed between us, drawing us together, irresistibly, deliberately, until my lips were on hers, moist, full and softly parted. My heart pumped and my breath came shallow as I felt her fingers in my hair, her arms pulling me tight.

And as abruptly as it began, she broke away, embarrassed, fumbling in her purse for her keys. "I'm sorry," she said, flustered, "I knew I should've changed my shoes before I left the house."

"Don't blame yourself, Carly. The ground's littered with

stones. As long as you didn't turn an ankle or worse, no real harm done." I took her by both arms and held her like that until she looked up into my face. "I'm not sorry for what happened. I've been—"

"Don't, Bryan, it's all right, it's my fault."

"There's nothing to blame anybody for. It had to happen sooner or later, Carly. I wanted it to happen. I just didn't expect it to be like this."

"No explanation needed, I understand." She pulled away from me. "Thanks for the coffee," she said, brightening and singling out her car key.

I moved around her and opened the car door. "You really should lock it, you know."

She scoffed. "Do you think anybody would really want to steal this rusty old bucket?"

"Not only that, somebody could be hiding in the back—uh oh, there's that cyn—"

"I've heard about such things happening," she said smiling, "and you do have a point."

"Well, I'm glad you've seen the light." I helped her in. "Can I give you a call in a couple of days? I mean, to make sure your ankle hasn't swollen up."

"Of course, doctor. And thanks for meeting me. As for 'seeing the light,' *I'll* decide when I see it...*if* I ever see it."

"Whoops," I said, closing the door and standing aside as she started up, backed out and pulled away, giving me a final wave.

Driving home, I felt elated as I relived the afternoon with her. I passed over the uncomfortable memory of our little confrontation and concentrated on our kiss, not that I could really think of anything else. She didn't resist me, not for a second. Sure, at the end, she had to break away; we couldn't stand there all evening looking at each other. But the way her arms encircled me—well, that told me she was not only willing to kiss me, but she welcomed it, as well, unplanned as it was. Now the icy wall she put between us was shattered forever. That single kiss thawed the miles of frozen tundra separating us. I could still taste the sweetness of her breath, feel the moist warmth of her lips. I only wished I knew how deeply she'd been affected.

I began to hum one of Sam's tunes until I captured the melody, then I sang: "You made me love you, I didn't want to do it, I didn't want to do it...." I didn't know the rest of the words, so I whistled as much of the song as I could remember.

I never did tell her I was an attorney, I remembered, as I had intended to do. It wasn't really so important, but I didn't want her to think I hadn't been up front with her when she finally does learn the truth. She might wonder what else I was holding back.

At the same time, how much did I really know about her? Where was she from? Every time I tried to learn something about her, she managed to side-step my questions and turn the conversation in a different direction. She did say she was what, twenty-five years old? Where had she been until now? Why was she still in school? Where did she get that touch of class that was so obvious in her manner and speech?

There was something mysterious about that girl, something I couldn't put my finger on. But in time I'd get my answers. She couldn't hide from me forever.

I switched on my headlights and cut over to a main artery. I tried whistling the tune to the last song we heard, but I couldn't recall it. Maybe, I thought, just maybe, I was an ADD victim and didn't know it.

Chapter 13

You Made Me Love You. I couldn't get the song out of my head as I drove through early morning traffic to the north side of town. And I couldn't stop humming it, either. I was consumed with memories of the day before with Bryan. I had a restless night and trouble falling asleep, recalling his lips on mine, his arms around me like a vice, holding me as if he'd never let go. I hated to admit it to myself, but I did love being in his embrace, loved the feeling of being wanted and desired by him. The happiness I felt at that moment frightened me.

For hours I had lain there replaying the afternoon in my mind. I thought of the things Bryan said and remembered the ever-changing expressions I saw in his eyes. I noticed his mannerisms, the way he nervously twisted a swizzle stick when he wanted to ask a question. Everything I remembered thrilled me. Yet, despite it all, I was restless and fearful. It was dangerous to be so happy. Reaching for happiness was like climbing a high mountain, one that could give you an exhilarating view of the world one moment, and in the next, without warning, could send you plummeting to the depths of an unimaginable hell. It was always better, safer, to smother such feelings whenever they threatened to bring down your defenses against them. Happiness carried the risk of pain. I don't know about others, but for myself, not seeking it and avoiding it altogether when it seemed to present itself made my life simpler. A boring life that way, I suppose, but not if I keep myself occupied with work or distracted in some way.

I couldn't help feeling anxious, maybe from the sheer exhaustion of thinking. I finally fell into a deep sleep with dreams of Bryan. In the morning I woke up refreshed and cheerful and with a joy in my heart that refused to be suppressed.

None of it made sense, not the talk, not the kiss, not his face which haunted me even now as I drove along— least of all, could I make sense of my own vacillating emotions which, much to my chagrin, sabotaged my reason and undermined my will.

At two sharp I arrived, at my destination, turning off the street onto the cracked asphalt driveway between two fieldstone pillars crowned with marble lion heads glistening with frost in the cold afternoon sunlight. I followed the curved drive under an overarching bridge of shedding Norwegian maple trees— in the hot summer a veritable tunnel of dark, cool shade— past the stiff, brown remains of flower beds laid low, toward the house, which stood like a monument to some long-past age of pomp and glory. A rectangular, three-story mass of white limestone and red sandstone trim, it conveyed an impression of dignity and grace, with its Corinthian four-column portico projecting from the building's center and its tiara-like, white balustrade across the roof.

But its opulence and formality were an illusion created by distance, I knew, as I drew close and wheeled past the weathered exterior and around to the back where I pulled up to the garages and parked my car. Earlier, I called my mother to tell her I'd be coming over to visit but wouldn't be staying for lunch.

'But, Carla, surely you can spare an hour or two. Your father and I hardly ever see you lately.'

'I'd love to, Mother, but I can't. I'm pressed for time and have an appointment at three with one of the professors at school.'

I unbuckled my seat belt and checked my hair in the mirror before grabbing my purse and sliding off the seat. I adjusted my corduroy jacket over my jeans and made my way across the grounds to the main entrance under the overhanging porch on the north side of the house.

Inside the central hall, hanging from the domed ceiling of the upper floor, the cut-glass chandelier flung its scattered light about, dimly illuminating the walls and the portraits of family members, many of whom lay buried in the niche graveyard in the southwest corner of the property. Directly ahead, rising between glass-smooth banisters I had so often slid down as a child, lay the broad staircase leading up to my bedroom, where my canopy bed still stood, its ruffled bedcovers laden with dolls I'd pampered over the years, where I played house and drank imaginary tea from cups, with an imaginary playmate I called Dottie.

More than a mansion, more than a house, it was a home, the home I loved with its eternally nostalgic smells of wood and stone, of plaster and carpeting and varnish and a thousand subtle fragrances and scents I couldn't name but could recognize as belonging to this singular place where I was born and raised, where love filled the house with warmth and happiness, where I ran laughing through rooms playing hide-and-seek with my younger brother Warren, who died at the age of seven from a congenital heart condition. I remembered both of us peeking through the railing to the people below, elegantly dressed in tuxedos and gowns, carrying on whispered conversations and sipping from champagne glasses while a string quartet played soft music in the background.

The polished oak floor creaked underfoot as I walked past the staircase through the vaulted hall to the archway.

"Hi, Mother," I said, entering the living room. A pearly light filtered through the sheers and fell across the furniture— the overstuffed armchairs and sofas that still looked comfortable, despite their age.

"Carla!" my mother called out, holding up the hem of her dress and shuffling across the room to me, pulling me in close and hugging my cheek to her own. "It's been two weeks since you've been here, dear. I was beginning to worry."

"Mother, I've been calling nearly every day."

"I know, still, it's not the same as seeing you. Will you have some tea? I already have the water on. Your father will be down shortly."

"I can't stay long," I said, strolling further into the room and touching my fingertip to the trembling gold leaves of the *tree of fortune* atop the grand piano gracing an alcove. "I have a class meeting in the school library."

"Surely, dear, you have time to join me for a cup of tea. You know I always have it this time of day."

I turned and smiled at my mother, at the frail woman who stood uncertainly before me, twisting the end of a lacy handkerchief tucked in the gauzy sleeve of her white blouse and trying to smile through a powdery mask I know she put on especially for me.

"Of course, Mother, I'd love some."

"Fine. Make yourself comfortable and I'll be right back."

"How's Dad doing?" I asked, but my mother was already out of earshot.

Sauntering across to the windows, I pulled aside the curtain and gazed out through the portico to the south side of the house. The hardwood trees dotting the lawn, their ragged branches nearly stripped, seemed to reach to the sky for relief from their loneliness and the cold. Even the little plot of ground squared with a wrought iron fence where my grandfather— builder of the mansion, and other family members lay buried— even it looked abandoned and forlorn without the sheltering green foliage of the trees.

Physically, nothing had changed, really. All was as it had once been, except that it had grown a little older, a little shabbier and undeniably sadder. A pall, palpable as crepe, hung over everything, and everything seemed as forlorn and sapped of life as the gardens crushed white by the frost on the south lawn. The joy that had once infused the grounds, the air, the very walls, seemed to have deserted the place. I let go the curtain, peeled off my jacket and made a slow retreat to one of the two armchairs across from the massive fieldstone fireplace that dominated the room. Draping my jacket over the arm of the chair, I plopped myself down. Dust motes rose around me in the light and I watched them rise toward the beamed ceiling.

As always, whenever I came home to visit, pangs of guilt assailed me and made me want to escape, to pick up and run away from the gloom and the melancholy that had invaded and taken over the house.

Moments later my mother returned, walking stiffly with a silver tray carefully balanced before her. "I put a few cookies on a plate, dear. You might like to try them. I made them myself." She placed the tray on the cocktail table between us and smiled as she sat primly sideways on the edge of her chair and reached forward to fill our cups.

"What?" I said, "none for Dottie?"

"Pardon me, dear?"

"Nothing, Mother, just something between me and myself."

My mother lifted an eyebrow. "Yes, well, with most people, that sort of thing usually comes a little later in life." She stirred sugar into her cup. "Things certainly aren't quite the same now that Milly's not with us full time."

"You've cut her hours?"

"We have her in only two days a week now. Since your father's had to give up work, we've decided to reduce expenses. Not that we couldn't afford the expense if we wished…. Look, dear, I even made these cookies myself, and they're every bit as good as Milly's, if I do say so myself…. Lemon?"

I shook my head. "No, Mother, I said, troubled by what she said. "Are you managing okay? If you really need—"

My mother waved me off with her teaspoon. "I'm fine, dear. I'm stronger than I look, I can assure you. As you know, of course, taking up the slack, so to speak, wasn't easy at first, but I've become quite adept at attending to what needs to be done. Naturally, there's always something left undone, but, on the whole, I've adjusted rather well, I think. Oddly enough, I feel better for it, much better than I could have ever anticipated."

"You did keep your doctor's appointment yesterday, didn't you?"

"Of course. My glucose is a little high, but quite manageable. Doctor Epstein says my health is fine, overall. More exercise would be beneficial, naturally, and he made me promise to walk more. In this house, it's an easy promise to keep."

"And how about Dad? Any improvement?"

"The oncologist isn't optimistic, and with good reason. He refuses to undergo treatment. He's such a stubborn man. Just this morning, I said to him…."

I well knew my father's stubbornness. A thin man, small and sinewy, but with a grim determination that showed in his fierce expression and penetrating eyes, he was not one given to taking orders well. Whether it was his medical condition or business or politics or anything else, he believed only what he wanted to believe and did only what he wanted to do.

"...and it couldn't come at a worse time, this health problem. Even before the foreign companies broke into our markets, business had been slow, but it's slowly improving, I think. I'm sure it will pick up again before long. I have to believe it will."

I couldn't help frowning. "Mother, that's terrible."

"His worry over the business isn't helping his condition any, and of course it's understandable. Why, just yesterday...."

'Just yesterday.' Well, it seemed like yesterday, her father sitting across from her in the parlor discussing her coming marriage to Bertram:

"I believe Bertram will make you a good husband," he said. "I know he's somewhat older than you, but—"

"Dad, you don't have to convince me. I said I'm going to marry him. I know it's what you want, what Mother wants."

"Not for my sake, Carly, understand that. I don't want you entering this union if you don't want to. And of course I couldn't force you to if I tried. But consider: Bert's educated and ambitious. I have no doubt he loves you very much."

"Yes, Dad. And of course, his father owns Lehigh Manufacturing, which would be a very nice company to merge with ours. We could become rich beyond our wildest dreams. We could become Wall Street royalty again."

He stood up, stiffening. "Young lady, that was uncalled for."

"Maybe, Dad, but it's true, isn't it? Wouldn't it make us a stronger company, a better competitor, if I married Bertram Kirby the Second? Or is it the Third?"

He glared down at me. "You're not marrying him for my sake, are you?"

I hesitated. "I'm sorry, Dad. No, I'm marrying him

because… because I do love him."

"Then that's all that matters. There's no more to discuss."

I loved Bertram, I felt sure, but why did I feel uncomfortable saying it? Why did the thought of marriage frighten me so? He certainly was good to me, loved me and treated me with the utmost respect. True, he was headstrong, very much like my father, and he was a little reckless, especially zooming around town in his Mercedes convertible. At times his jealousy created arguments between us, but we always settled them amicably enough.

He was an ivy-league college graduate and was every girl's dream catch, if they could ever catch him— rich, handsome, cultured and talented. From the moment he met me at my 'Coming Out' party, he pursued me relentlessly. It was almost a foregone conclusion we'd be married one day….

"…and it's affecting him in so many ways. Since your father's been taken ill and unable to keep up, the company has taken on new strategies. Highly professional people are involved. Nevertheless, he still worries, and perhaps with good reason." She paused to sip her tea. "Of course, we're not as well off as we were, Carla, but we're certainly comfortable enough. And if worse ever comes to worse, we have considerable assets."

I looked around doubtfully. "Oh, Mother, I hope you're not just saying that."

"It disturbs me to see him so unhappy. It's awful enough to watch him swirling his drink and staring out the window to his father's grave, saying nothing, just staring and thinking whatever a man thinks at such times. I never say anything but I know he's worried about me and what will happen to me should his condition worsen. I've lived with the man too long not to know his feelings."

"He's always been in control. Now, with his health a problem, and the comp—"

"Yes. And you."

"Me? Still? I thought he was getting over it. Hasn't he accepted the fact that I'm all grown up and want to be on my own? I want to make my own way in the world and not simply be known as the daughter of Edward Edmond Miller?"

"Don't be upset, dear. He—" She set her cup down and pressed a finger to her lips. "Here he is now," she whispered.

"Hi, Dad," I said, bouncing out of my chair and meeting him in the archway with a quick hug and kiss on the cheek.

He held out his drink to avoid spilling it. "Carly," he said, his colorless eyes sparkling in their watery pouches behind rimless glasses. "It's good to see you."

"And you, but Dad, should you be drinking, I mean, with all the medications you're taking?"

"Nonsense. They haven't hurt me yet, have they?"

I wrapped an arm around him, stroking his shoulder under the smooth silk of his robe, and walked with him across the room. "So how are you feeling overall?"

"Fine, just fine," he said, patting my arm and moving away. Setting his drink on the fireplace mantel, he stood with his hands clasped behind his back, facing my mother and me. Around his neck hung a loose, white scarf that draped down over his thin frame. "Tell me, Carly, how is school?"

"Very good, Dad, so far," I said, picking up my cup. "It's a lot of work, but I'm enjoying it." I bit into a cookie and took a sip of tea. "Delicious," I said, glancing toward my mother. "Oatmeal."

"And work?" he said. "Still with the restaurant?"

"Oh, sure. With my tips I know I make more than I could anywhere else. The most important thing is that I can make up my own hours to accommodate my school schedule. And of course, working so close to the college makes it so much more convenient than working anywhere else."

"I'm sure it does," he said, taking up his drink and looking away.

"Carla," my mother said, "let me be perfectly frank. Your father is not happy with your situation. And, to be perfectly honest, neither am I."

I tightened. "Mother, we've been through this before."

"Where you live. The school you're attending—"

"They're perfectly fine, Mother. I just explained—"

My father raised his hand and looked toward my mother. "I can speak for myself." Turning to me, he said, "The neighborhood is not safe. I know it well, and I have good reason to be concerned. Allow me to be blunt: the school is not— shall we say, of the first rank. And it grieves me to think of my daughter, with all her intelligence and talent, working in a restaurant as a waitress."

I lowered my head, stifling my frustration. "Dad, how many times do we have to go through this?"

"I'm sorry, Carly," he went on, "but you must know what's in my heart. To hide from the truth is a deception not worthy of any of us. So let me be clear. Your mother and I have discussed this thoroughly and we would prefer your living here. With us. You can have a comfortable life, anything you desire, as you once did. You will associate with the very best young men society has to offer. Or, if you insist, I can arrange for your transfer to any number of first-class universities. I still have influence—"

"Dad, please! I'm sorry to disappoint you, but I don't see myself as one of the 'upper crust.'"

He winced at my words.

"I know you and Mother want what you think is best for me, Dad. But can't you see, I'm happy with my life as it is."

"As a common waitress?"

"Yes," I said defiantly, "even, as you call it, a 'common' waitress. But remember, I don't intend to be one the rest of my life."

The glass trembled in his hand. "Well, then, will you allow me to find a university worthy of you."

"I'm perfectly satisfied with the school I'm in. Try to understand," I pleaded, looking at them both. "I don't want to be part of the world I put behind me four years ago, or is it five?"

Frustrated, he said, "Can I at least buy you a car, one that doesn't look like it's ready for the salvage yard, one you can depend on?"

"Please, Dad, my car's in excellent condition."

He rolled his eyes. "If only I could believe that."

My mother set her cup aside and rose to her feet. "Carla, is this all a part of—"

"Mother, no. I don't want to think about it, I don't want to discuss it, and I'd appreciate it if you never bring it up again."

"I'm sorry, dear. I didn't mean to bring up anything unpleasant and upset you."

I saw the firm set of my father's jaw as he gazed toward the window beyond which lay the graveyard where a place for him had already been reserved between his father and grandfather.

"I'm sorry," I said, reaching for my jacket. "I didn't come here to make a scene or get into an argument or cause any kind of trouble. I just want you to know I'm content where I'm at and with what I'm doing. And please remember, I'm always here if you need me." I glanced toward my mother's tortured face as I slipped on my jacket. "For whatever reason."

"We know that, dear," she said, stepping over and hugging me.

I walked over to my father, where he stood, with his back to me, still gazing outside. "Dad, I'm sorry. Please try to understand."

His voice sounded weary. "If nothing else, at least let me arrange for a weekly stipend to carry you so you don't have to work in a restaurant."

"Oh, Dad," I said, putting my arm around his shoulder and hugging him. "I would rather do it my way, really I would, but thank you again."

He turned sad eyes on me. "Carly, I don't understand."

"Please understand that I appreciate everything you've done for me and want to do for me, and know that I love you," I said. "I love you both very much."

Chapter 14

Saturday afternoon rolled around bright and cheerful, as I, feeling as bright and cheerful, rolled up to the curb in front of Carly's apartment. When I called her a few days earlier to ask how her ankle was healing up, she told me it was well enough to go on another excursion, if I was willing. Except for saying it wouldn't be another poolroom, she wouldn't tell me what she had in mind.

"Okay," I said, after she climbed into the car, "what's the big surprise today? Are we wrestling alligators?"

"Oooo, what an idea. Would you have the nerve?" she said, swinging toward me and flashing a mischievous smile.

I laughed. "Since we don't have them in this part of the country, you'll never know, will you?" I gave her a quick once-over. Obviously, she had nothing fancy in mind, judging by her jeans, long-sleeved tan blouse and light jacket. "Well?"

"Well what?"

"Directions, please," I said. "North, south, east or west?"

She pointed. "Thata way."

"That's west."

"I know that."

"Of course you do. Now do you mind telling me where we're going?"

"Promise you won't back out?"

"Do I need a gun?"

She laughed the same infectious laugh I first heard at Sam's restaurant. "No, no gun, just good taste."

"What, a restaurant?"

"Have you ever heard of Monet?"

"Of course. It's a song. I sang a couple of bars: Monet makes the world go 'round... Monet makes the world go round.... They use it in France, except there you get it in francs."

"Are you serious?"

"Don't I sound serious?"

She arched a fine, black eyebrow. "I mean Claude Monet."

"Oh, that Monet. If you were a real American, you'd have sounded out the 't.'"

"Well, I am part French."

"Oh, that's different. So where are we supposed to see this guy, this Monet."

"Stop being silly. Didn't you read about his display at the Albright Art Gallery this week? These are supposed to be some of the last works he did before he went totally blind."

"Totally blind?" I swung the wheel left and climbed the on-ramp to the expressway. "So, does that mean he was almost blind when he painted them?"

She turned serious. "I should have asked you first. If you don't want to go—"

"No, it's okay, I want to go."

"Really, Bryan, if you'd rather not—"

"Honest, I like art galleries. I really do like them. I enjoy them thoroughly."

"We can forget it, Bryan. I don't think you mean it."

"I mean it, I mean it. I swear it, I love art galleries. I love the artists: Van Gogh, Picasso, all of them, even the guy who dribbles different colored paint like silly string all over the canvas."

"Now you're being sarcastic, aren't you?"

"Me? Never. I'm just trying to convince you that I appreciate art and know a thing or two about it. I want to go, definitely… But would you like to stop for a sandwich or something first?"

"Oh, I should have told you, I already had lunch. Didn't you?"

"I was only thinking of you. I had a late breakfast," I lied, hoping my stomach wouldn't rumble too loud.

"Oh, good. I was so intent on surprising you that I forgot to mention it. We would've had a hard time squeezing it in." She glanced at her watch. "It's past one-thirty and our appointment is for two o'clock."

"You're kidding. You mean you had to make an appointment?"

"Oh, yes. This is a very popular exhibit. I understand they're breaking records. His 'Gardens at Giverny' paintings are renowned."

"I've seen a few of them. Lots of purple flowers all bunched together, if I remember correctly."

"Yes, and these are the actual paintings. Can you believe it? I can't wait to see them. The *actual* oil paintings!"

"Oh, the *actual* oil paintings! Wow. I can't wait, either."

She looked askance, suspicious I might be putting her on, but all she saw on my face was my fixed, bland smile.

I tried to work up a little sincere enthusiasm, if for no other reason than to keep from spoiling her pleasure. Art was something I had a problem with. Realism I loved; I marveled at the incredible attention to detail, the realistic rendering of life, the subtle and sometimes not so subtle use of color. In short, I could make sense of it, but the abstract stuff totally confused me. A lot of it was colorful, but still…. Was I supposed to take the word of 'experts' and believe paintings like Picasso's Guernica were really important works? All those fractured, distorted images may be intended to symbolize death and destruction, but really, was that it? And Modigliani: what kind of symbolism was represented in his paintings of long faces, flat and expressionless as death masks? At the same time, and for reasons I couldn't understand, I did like Dali and his melting clocks and such. Maybe I simply wasn't intellectually ready for the 'classics.'

Aside from what I said, I wanted to stay within Carly's good graces. I'd almost ruined myself with her the last time we were at Sam's, talking about school.

"Should be exciting," I said, wheeling into the parking lot outside the gallery.

"There," she said pointing, "someone's pulling out."

"My lucky day," I said, smiling to cover my sarcasm.

We parked, walked across the lot and climbed a bank of marble stairs worthy of the Greek Parthenon itself.

Once inside, Carly presented the tickets, and we were directed to an elderly woman with a chalky face etched with time lines, and wearing a blond wig. Her glittery gown made her look as if she were going to a fancy ball. She was handing out earphones and a small tape cartridge to the people lined up to go inside.

"You have to let me pay you for these tickets," I said,

guiding Carly by the arm.

"Oh, no. This was my surprise, so it's my treat."

"We'll talk about it later." I took the earphones from the woman.

"As you'll see," the woman said, handing Carly hers, "the paintings are numbered and synchronized with the narration."

"Oh, you mean like painting by the numbers," I said, "only this is looking by the numbers. Or is it listening by the numbers?"

The woman's long face turned frigid.

Carly pulled me along. "That was uncalled for," she whispered, slipping on her earphones.

"What? What did I say?" I said, looking surprised.

"Bryan!"

"Thin-skinned people who take themselves so seriously and can't take a little kidding are doomed to a life of misery," I said. "And they deserve it," I added, falling in step with her.

I tried to hide the disappointment on my face as we passed from painting to painting. Carly, on the other hand, ooohed and ahhhed at every single one of them. After a few minutes I slipped off my earphones and studied the canvases, while Carly, standing beside me and staring intently at each masterpiece, concentrated on every word pouring into her ears. I had to literally pull her away from a few.

Coming full circle to the end of the display, we turned in our equipment to the same woman who had handed it out.

"It was a lovely display," Carly said, handing over her earphones. "I thoroughly enjoyed it."

"Thank you, it pleases us to know you enjoyed the

exhibition," the woman said with a smile, watching Carly move on.

When she turned back and met my eyes, her smile turned into an instant scowl of recognition.

Scowling back, I pinched my nose with the fingers of one hand and watched the woman's nostrils flare as I held the earphones like a dead mouse between my thumb and forefinger of the other hand and dropped them into her trembling palm.

Her eyes popped and she looked as if she were choking when I moved away.

"Wasn't that fantastic?" Carly said, turning and taking my arm when I caught up with her.

"Actually, I was hoping to see an alligator or something swimming around in one of those ponds, but it was just one watery garden scene after the other."

"Well, that's just it. Didn't you see the changes, the gradual progression as his eyesight failed?"

"For better or worse?"

She pulled me up short with her sudden stop. "You didn't like it."

"I didn't say that."

"You don't have to. Your remarks alone—"

"Are honest ones. Do you want me to pretend it was a great display? All that gobbledegook on the tape." I mocked in a song-like voice:

"'One will note the shadowed recesses, which reflect the mental depression and dark fate this great artist faced with his failing sight. Note the blurring of—'"

"That's your opinion," she said.

"Right, my opinion. Which of course means I'm not one of the enlightened ones. Now, if something in those paintings impressed you, fine. I didn't. I've seen other work by him. I really have, a hundred times better. Why they chose to send these particular paintings over— is beyond me." I wanted to say they probably sent these over because if the ship carrying them from France sank along the way, it would be no great loss.

"I don't want to discuss it anymore," she said, freeing her arm and strutting ahead of me.

From another passageway emerged a pasty-faced young man wearing pearl-framed sunglasses and sporting an unruly head of dark hair streaked with orange. He had a knapsack slung over his bony shoulder and floppy sneakers on his feet. He swerved in the nick of time to avoid a collision with Carly.

"Wasn't it simply delicious?" he said, coming alongside of her and smiling broadly. "Did you perceive the subtle gradation of colors, his sensitivity to light?"

Carly looked at him quizzically.

"The exhibit," he said. "Monet. I was standing behind you."

"Oh, that, yes," she said, shooting an over-the-shoulder look of disdain toward me, stumbling after her.

"The rich texture of the wisteria and the irises," the young man gushed. "Don't you agree? The peacefulness of diffused, almost hallowed light, imbuing the paintings? Couldn't you just feel it, feel the subtle, gentle crush of the flowers?" He hugged himself. "Couldn't you almost… smell them?"

"The smell was there, all right I interjected.

"Carly shot me a cold look."

"As a burgeoning artist myself, I can perhaps more fully appreciate the talent of the man. See the water lilies! How they dominate yet harmonize with the foliage surrounding the pond," he oozed, his spidery fingers weaving a mental tapestry. "Notice their symbolic tranquility and the melding of color, so fluid in its stillness. It leaves one with such a grand sense of solace and inner peace."

I grabbed Carly's arm and steered her away.

"Okay, I guess I'm outvoted," I said. "I defer to your superior aesthetic sensibilities and promise to withhold my opinions until such time I'm better informed in the esoteric matters of art."

"Stop it, Bryan, stop making fun of me. I suggested this because I thought you might like the exhibit. I guess I made a mistake."

I could see she was genuinely hurt. "Come on, Carly, don't take it that way. The fact is, I suspect there may be something to these works I can't quite comprehend, so I'll tell you what— I'll hold my final judgment till a later time, how's that?"

"Don't try to pacify me if you don't mean it, Bryan."

"I'm not, I swear it," I said, opening the car door for her.

I climbed in on my side and pulled away, hoping I hadn't upset her too much. I had a way about me of doing it. At the same time, she seemed awfully sensitive to every damn word that fell from my lips, guarded or unguarded. Were we both unconsciously trying to sabotage our relationship? I wondered. Could we do a better job of it if we tried?

We drove about a half mile in silence before she spoke again. "Lisa wants us to double date with her and a friend of hers. Are you interested?"

"Fine with me, but by the sound of your voice, you don't seem too pleased. Is it because of this afternoon, of what I've been saying?"

"No. Actually, it has to do with…."

"Do with what?"

"I suppose it's none of my business."

"What isn't?"

"I don't really have a right to…"

"To what, Carly, tell me, will you?"

"In a nutshell, I don't think he's right for Lisa."

"Why not?"

"For one thing, I think he's too old for her, forty or maybe even older, although I didn't make it sound that bad when I mentioned his age to her. Other than what I can see I don't know much about him, except for what Lisa tells me. And, naturally, to her he's the greatest thing since chocolate milk. Maybe I'm just overly concerned because she's so naïve, even though she's almost twenty and should know better, and… well, I hate to say it, but she's just too anxious to find somebody. I think she's afraid of being an old maid. Can you imagine, at her age, worrying about being an old maid? I can't help worrying about her."

"So you're willing to go on a date with them to judge for yourself."

"Am I wrong? I mean, to want to help her?"

"Suppose you don't think he's right for her. Can you be sure?"

"I'm sure I can be more objective about him than she can."

"I don't know if that proves anything, but let's do this: You set up a date and we'll see how it goes. Afterward you can decide whether you want to say anything or not." I reached over and took her hand in mine and squeezed it. "Okay?"

She smiled and squeezed back. "Any suggestions where we can go?"

"I got an idea: how about a nice art—owww," I cried as her fingernails dug into me.

Chapter 15

With my face half-lathered with shaving cream, I rushed out of the bathroom to catch the phone.

"This is short notice, I know, but will you be available Saturday afternoon?"

"Who is this, please?"

"Oh, come on, Bryan?"

"Pardon me?"

A sigh. "It's me, Carly."

"Charley? Charley who? I don't know any Charley."

"Not Charley. Carly. Carly Miller. Now Bryan, stop it."

"Oh, Carly. Hi, Carly. Sorry, my hearing is getting bad. Do you think I could become a good musician? I mean, if you can't see and be a famous painter, well then, if you can't hear—"

"Funny, Bryan, very funny. You can't give it up, can you? You just can't leave well enough alone, can you? Are you done? Can we talk now?"

"Of course, of course."

"Are you sure?"

"Sure I'm sure."

"All right then. So, is Saturday workable for you? Saturday afternoon?"

"Saturday afternoon? That should be fine, why?"

"Would you like to visit the zoo? Or do you have something against zoos?"

"Are you serious?"

"It was Lisa's idea, not mine."

"Oh, you mean the double-date you mentioned."

"Exactly."

"If that's her idea of a romantic setting, it's okay with me. What time?"

"Be at the apartment by two?"

"Will we be getting something to eat afterwards?'

"I should think so."

*　*　*　*　*

At two sharp on Saturday I pulled up in front of Carly's apartment and was about to get out when I saw her strutting down the sidewalk to the car. She was wearing a neat pair of designer jeans, and a navy-blue corduroy jacket over a white turtleneck sweater.

"On the button," I said, stretching over and opening the door from the inside.

Carly slid in beside me. "Mr. Dependable."

"Better than Mr. Depends," I said, leaning over suddenly and planting a quick kiss on her cheek.

She blushed a rosy pink. "I'm glad we caught a nice day," she said. "Chilly, but nice and bright."

"Where's Lisa?"

"Oh, they'll meet us at the zoo parking lot. She had to pick up her friend?" To my puzzled look she said, "His car broke down. Anyway, that's the story he told her and the story she told me."

"Such things happen," I said, pulling away. "I seem to remember someone being stranded with a flat tire once. In a very inconvenient place." I glanced over slyly.

"That was for real. Lisa was very embarrassed telling me because she thinks I'll think he's only using her."

"She probably guesses how you feel about him and figures this is giving you more ammunition to use against her."

"Well, I can't say it hurts…."

The zoo parking lot wasn't at all crowded when we pulled in.

"There they are," Carly said, pointing, "standing next to Lisa's car."

I swung around and took a spot a few spaces away. Together, we climbed out and walked over. Lisa hugged Carly as if she hadn't seen her in a year, then shook my hand. I recognized her from the restaurant, of course, but she apparently didn't recognize me.

"Finally we meet," Lisa said.

"Face to face, anyway," I answered.

"Carly," she said, pulling her close by the arm, "This is David… David…"

"Campio," he finished.

"Campio, of course," Lisa said, embarrassed. "Lisa's my favorite roommate, David."

"Her only one," Carly said, touching the fingertips of his extended hand. "Pleased to meet you, David. And this is Bryan Perri."

I recognized him at once as the customer Lisa sat with in the restaurant booth, but I didn't let on. I shook hands, taking in at once the hair, black as crude oil, the dark roots of a clean-shaven face and the smallish eyes fixed on him. His smooth skin lent his face an oddly youthful cast.

"Well, shall we go in," Lisa said, arm-locking David and obviously excited as she led the way.

We wandered along the cement path, past a few mundane exhibits with animals that looked like wild pigs and goats, the four of us making small talk and commenting on anything of interest.

David, who at first seemed wary and withdrawn, began to relax and open up, albeit ever so gradually. He whistled up to an eagle roosting near the top of its iron cage. "Baldy must be deaf," he said. "Could pop him off easy with a pea shooter if I had one."

To a peacock strutting by and spreading his colorful tail, he called, "Hey, showoff, why don'cha join a burlesque show with the rest of the fan dancers?" Lisa smiled over her shoulder at Carly and me, a few steps behind.

We passed a lone zebra nibbling at a bale of hay. "Hey, Zeeb, what did you do to get those hoosegow duds, rob a store?"

He laughed and we smiled politely. I picked up on the 'hoosegow duds.' No doubt about it, using outdated words like that proved he was a heck of a lot older than he appeared to be.

Wandering along, we stopped by the polar bears flopped on a table rock across the deep pit between them. "Whatsa matter, too warm for you guys?" David called. "If you can't 'bare' the heat, take off your coats, why doncha?" He turned to Lisa. "Get it, Lisa, 'bare' the heat?" He leaned over the railing and called to another bear walking toward the pit. "Hey, Pigeon Toes, did you hear what happened when the two Eskimos kissed...? They got sniffilis."

"Isn't David witty?" Lisa said, beaming.

Carly and I exchanged quick glances. "He sure is," Carly said. "Very witty."

We moved around a few people staring through the thick bars of the elephant enclosure. Frankie the Indian elephant stood swishing his trunk back and forth, waiting for someone to throw him a treat.

"Oh, David, we should have bought some peanuts at the concession stand," Lisa said, disappointed. "Elephants love peanuts. Maybe we can get some before we come back around this way. I just love the zoo, don't you, Carly?"

"It's been a long time since I've been here," Carly said. "Somehow it's not as big as I remember it."

"Hey, look at that," David cried, pointing to the elephant. "Holy smoke, is that Frankie ever taking a mean dump... like bowling balls. And look at that waterfall with it."

Carly turned away embarrassed.

David laughed. "Man, what a commercial for one of them companies like Ex-Lax! They could make a fortune. Maybe I'll write a letter and get a commission from it." He laughed again and turned to Lisa. "Remind me."

"Let's go, David," Lisa said, tugging at his arm.

"Hey, take it easy, take it easy. Can't you see I had a brainstorm? In case you didn't notice, I got a business head for making up this kind of stuff. In fact, I even got an idea on how the church can make a few extra bucks. And some companies, too"

When all of us turned blank faces toward him, he went on as

if we asked to hear it.

"Yeah, that's right, how the church can make a fast buck, and I think it's a great idea. Take the Bible, for instance. Lots of writing, lots of stories we all heard about, even people like me who don't go to church much. How about one with what's- his-name, you know, where his wife got turned into a pile of salt because she looked cock-eyed at God or something…"

"Lot," I said, instantly sorry I opened my mouth.

"Lot…yeah, he's the guy. So here's my idea: If the church starts taking advertisements to put in the Bible like the way almost every other magazine does, it could make a fortune, I'm sure. Like right here what I said about Lot, they could stick in an extra page from some company that makes salt. Morton's is a big one, ain't it? They could clean up, both of them, the church and Morton's. Well…?" he said looking at us from one face to another. '…what do you think?"

We all nodded and smiled politely.

"And how about when Samson beat all those guys' heads in with a donkey's skull. Some bodybuilding or vitamin company could say…" he extended his arm and flexed his bicep "…You, too, can have Samson's muscles. Or something like that.

"Somebody said the Bible sells more than any other book every year. Can you imagine the profits a bunch of advertisements between those pages could bring in? A fortune, I'll bet. And some boat company, too, with a picture of Noah and all the animals in his—Hey, wait up! I ain't finished talking yet!"

Lisa hung back, but Carly and I were already shuffling ahead.

David pouted a little bit, but eventually he and Lisa caught up to us. When we came to a water buffalo with its typically runny nose, David called, "Hey, what's the matter, got a bad case of hay fever?" He turned to Lisa. "How about *that* for a commercial? I wish we'd of brought a camera so I could take a picture and send it to one of them companies. Can't you see it now? A picture of this ugly animal with his snotty nose and the words under it saying, 'Allergy season got you, too? Try Whatever.'" He clenched a tight fist. "Oh, man, am I good or am I good? I'll bet anything I can cash in big time with stuff like this."

Lisa glanced nervously over her shoulder, apparently to see how Carly and I were reacting to her boyfriend. We were already aware David was an obnoxious jerk, but we put on smiling faces for her benefit.

When we came to the hippo enclosure, David stretched his neck. "Will you look-see over there? Take a gander at that rump," he said, staring intently until he had everyone's attention, then turned and stared at Lisa's backside. "Must run in the family," he said, slapping his thigh and laughing so hard he started to cough and choke.

Lisa's face flushed to match her red hair. "It's not funny, David, not one bit."

"Aww, whatsa matter, Baby, can't you take a little joke?"

Carly and I looked away to spare Lisa's embarrassment.

We strolled along until we came to the reptile house. "Anybody interested in seeing this?" Lisa asked.

Shrugging, we followed each other inside. The rancid smell of fetid water made Carly feel nauseated. "I don't think I can take much of this," she whispered to me.

"Hey, gruesome," David called down to an alligator stretched out on a slate beach, "ever think of seeing a dentist to get those teeth straightened?" He looked around, grinning, and lapping up the titters of other spectators who turned their attention to him. "Hey, ugly," he called to another, "I saw your old man advertised on Amazon last week. A whole bunch of your relatives, in fact. Must have been a family reunion. Ha ha. At least it proves you guys got souls. Get it? Soles," he said, pointing to his shoe. Basking in the limelight of his momentary celebrity, he called again. "Which one of you guys is Percy? Get it? Purse-y. Like your mama's purse-y." He laughed. "Man, I could go for a belt right now. A belt from you, and one from you and one from you," he said, pointing to each alligator staring up to him with hungry eyes and gaping jaws. Turning to Lisa he said out of the side of his mouth, "Man, oh man, how many ways can I say it, am I good or am I good? I got talent coming out of the gazoo."

Carly and I had already withdrawn and Lisa looked like she was putting a little space between herself and David.

"David, the others are leaving. Let's go."

He glanced around for admiring faces. "Yeah, sure, let's get out of the luggage department," he said, taking her arm and moving away.

"David, I wish you wouldn't do that," she said, trying to hurry to catch up to Carly and me, already a distance ahead.

"Do what?" David said peevishly. "What?"

"Make comments about everything."

"Those are jokes. Didn't you hear them people standing around, the way they were laughing? How about them clapping right about when you pulled me away? Man, I had an audience. Eating right out of the palm of my hand. Maybe I missed my calling in life, in fact, I know it. Move over Seinfeld. David the comic is here."

"Yes, David, you were funny, but it's a little embarrassing

183

for me. I mean, I want you to make a good impression on Carly and Bryan, not to act like a clown."

"A clown! Hey, there's a difference, you know. A clown makes a jerk out of himself to get a laugh, mugs and throws himself all over the place. I was doing stand-up stuff like you see on television. Professional. And strictly off the cuff, too."

"Oh, I know, David, but I mean… couldn't you save it till they get to know you a little better?"

"Hey, I know who I am. If they don't, too bad for them."

"Shhh, David," she said, glancing around nervously, "they might hear you."

Actually, we did hear him but we pretended not to. Together, the four of us passed through to the lion house. The strange jungle odors made Carly feel dizzy, and the occasional roars echoing off the walls hurt her ears and frightened her. A few of the lions, leopards and other more exotic cats lay sleeping or stared out at us stupor-like. We moved on to the aviary holding thousands of colorful, chirping, twittering birds flitting around inside their cages before passing through to the primate house.

The tile walls echoed the pandemonium of ear-piercing cries as we entered and stopped to watch a family of screeching monkeys swinging from ropes and trapezes in frantic pursuit of each other, stopping momentarily to stare at the audience before resuming their frenzied game of chase.

Moving along, we paused to view a forlorn group of monkeys gazing up to us with their large, sad eyes. "Aren't they adorable?" Lisa said.

Carly moved closer to me. "They seem so human. It makes you want to cuddle them."

The baboons seemed different from all the other primates. A few searched the floor, picking up tidbits and nibbling on them.

Others sat quietly on their haunches, or got up lazily to move to another spot. Two gazed through the bars defiantly, as if challenging us.

"They may look harmless," I said, "but those baboons can rip you to pieces with those teeth. And given half a chance, they would."

Carly shuddered. "They don't look harmless to me at all," she said. "In fact, they look pretty ferocious."

"Hey, looks kinda like you, Lisa," David said, casting a mock appraisal her way. "A little around the eyes and a lot from behind." He laughed. "Whoa, get a load of that red butt, will you?"

The blood drained from Lisa's face as she ducked away.

"Hey, ugly, that's some case of hemorrhoids you got there," David called to the baboon exhibiting itself near the wall. "Better get yourself some Preparation H; you can sure use it. A whooole lot of it. And while you're at it, try getting a little more fiber into that banana diet of yours. How 'bout some Metamucil; that should do the trick." He broke himself up laughing again. "How's that for a couple of great advertisements for them companies? Preparation H and Metamucil, a double-header. I'll bet they'd sell in a minute. Man," he said, punching his fist into his hand, "I betcha I could make a fortune in this business if I put my mind to it and somebody'd give me a break." He looked around. "Hey, hey, and don't nobody get it in their head to go stealing my ideas, neither."

"Let's move and get out of here," I said, breaking away.

"Wait a minute, for crying out loud," David called after me, "I want to see the chimps. I paid good money to get in. What's the big rush anyway?"

We stopped in front of the chimpanzee cage, housing Eddie, a long time resident and the most famous of all the primates in the zoo.

"Hey, Eddie, where's Cheetah?" David called to him.

Eddie glared back. Carly and I couldn't avoid exchanging disgusted glances. Lisa tried to put a little more space between herself and David.

"They say one of these monkeys has got the strength of ten guys," David said, "but I don't know if it's true or not."

Why not climb inside and find out, I thought to myself.

"Hey, Eddie," David called, "a little lonesome in there? Oooh, too bad, but with a sour-puss like that I can understand why." He made a mocking face. "Oh, you want a staring contest, eh? That's it, stare. Go on, try and outstare me, let's see you do it, you smelly, freaky—"

Eddie suddenly sprang from his perch on a wall shelf to the narrow bars of his cage, where he clung hands and feet looking down at us from about three feet above our heads.

Startled, we all jumped away from the brass rail, set a few feet back from the cage.

Eddie bared his teeth and burst forth with a shrill, yelping cry.

David bellied up to the railing again. "Yeah, go tell it to Tarzan, you ugly, bald-headed tree-swinging—"

A sudden stream of hot urine shot from Eddie, spraying David square in the face and spilling down over his shoulders.

Momentarily stunned, David fell back. "You sonofabitch!" he cried, sputtering and flailing, trying to escape the hosing bath drenching him from head to foot. "You dirty sonofabitch!"

Eddie bounded aro und his cage, slapping and pounding the walls, creating pandemonium in the building as he swung and leaped in a dizzying pattern, baring his teeth and shrieking insanely along with a chorus of monkeys shrieking in their cages.

And Lisa shrieking, too. "David! David!"

"Get away," he shouted, staggering around, cursing and pulling at his face, "get away from me!"

For a moment all the onlookers stood rigid, totally stunned by the surprise attack, then gradually giggled and laughed until they burst out laughing hysterically.

When we finally snapped out of our disbelief, the three of us surrounded David, yanked him back and hustled him out of the primate house and down the path toward our cars. Lisa clung to his arm, trying to comfort him, but David wouldn't be comforted. He continued to curse Eddie and the zoo.

He pulled against Lisa. "Let me go, let me go back! I'll kill that crowd of sonsabitches in there laughing at me, every goddamned one of them, and every goddamned fuckin' animal in the fuckin' joint with them." His raging voice was choked with tears.

Lisa held him tight and I stepped in to help. "Come on, David," I said. "You have to get out of these clothes. They're soaked."

"That sonofabitchin Eddie! I'm comin' back, I tell you. I'm bringin' a shotgun and I'm gonna blow away every fuckin' hairy ape I see... that sonofabitch! That rotten— I'll kill every goddamned animal in sight, right down to those fuckin' squawking birds till there's nothing left to see but blood and guts splattered everywhere. I'll burn the fuckin' joint right to the ground!"

Lisa bumped and pulled him along, hushing him and placating him with soft words until we reached the parking lot, where she helped him into her car and apologized to us for ruining our afternoon.

Carly and I could still see him in the car, raving and frantically throwing his arms around as we stood and watched them drive away. Carly looked at me. "I can't say I'm sorry it happened," she said.

I smiled. "Couldn't happen to a nicer guy."

"He asked for it," Carly said giggling. "Did you see the expression on his face when Eddie sprayed him? He was so shocked he couldn't move."

"Not to mention the way he was sputtering and spitting. Did you see how it mixed in with the black stuff in his hair and ran down over his face? He must've colored his hair with black Kiwi shoe polish."

Walking back to the car we burst out laughing reliving Eddie's revenge and laughed all the way home.

Chapter 16

Carly and I took our usual booth near the corner of the restaurant. A song neither of us heard before was playing quietly in the background.

"Ah, my young friends," Sam said, sweeping up to us and drying his hands on his apron. "So good to see you both again."

Carly smiled up to him. "We couldn't stay away any longer, Sam."

"I'm so glad," he said, beaming. "What can I get you to drink first? Something hot, something cold…?"

"Coffee for me," I said.

Carly ordered tea.

"'Coffee and tea… 'at'sa for me… a rub adub adub a….' 'at'sa song, too, you know. We had crazy ones, same like today… *Mairzie Doats* and *Ce-ment Mixer*… So," he said, rubbing his hands together, "for dinner it'sa not too early, if you wish."

"Sam, if you knew what we've just been through," I said, "you'd bring us a gallon of Alka Seltzer."

His eyes opened wide. "A problem?"

"Not really a problem. Just an appetite killer."

"How about, then, some real Italian pizza. You ever taste white pizza?"

"White pizza?" Carly said. "Of course I've heard of it, and I think I had it once but I can't be sure."

"I've know I had it, but it was quite a while ago. I remember

189

it was good."

"Sure, you had it, Bryan, and maybe it's good or even very good, but you never get white pizza like here. And for Carly, maybe her first time, guaranteed delicious. No tomato sauce like the regular pizza, but a little Romano cheese, a little garlic, some olive oil, a little oregano, plus Caterina's secret spices. Hot from the oven. You love it."

"You know, that sounds good to me. What do you think, Carly?"

"If it's half as good—"

"Absolutely guaranteed," Sam said. "Okay then, coming up in twenty minutes or maybe a little bit more."

"We have time," I said, looking across at Carly and seeing her troubled face. "Still upset about this afternoon?"

"I suppose," she said, looking melancholy. "I'm really worried about Lisa."

I leaned back. "She probably feels pretty bad over the whole thing."

"Did you see how proud she was to introduce him to us? I know she was anxious to have me meet him, to have my approval— as if that means anything— and then—"

"The guy's a real idiot. It's not her fault."

"The way he humiliated her. So crude. I felt like slapping him. I almost said something, but I bit my tongue because I probably would have caused more harm than good."

I reached across the table and took her hand. "Look, Carly," I said, looking into her eyes, "it's beyond us, you and me. Nothing anybody can do will change what took a lifetime to create. Too bad, too. I have to say, though, beneath that slobby layer of ignorance, I believe he does have a measure of

190

cleverness."

Carly nodded. "Maybe if he had received some special attention way back to who knows when, he might have developed his 'cleverness' into something valuable."

"Ah, always hopeful," I said. "Anyway, Lisa's just going to have to drop him. It should be obvious to her now what kind of a guy she's dealing with."

"And I was right, Bryan. He is older than she is, much older than even I thought. He's fifty, if he's a day. Maybe sixty." Carly brightened. "This has to be the wake-up call she needed. I won't have to preach— that's what she's always accusing me of doing, if not outright messing with her love life."

"Well, Carly, people are funny. You never know."

She looked up sharply. "And what does that mean?"

Just then Sam stepped up with the coffee and tea. "Here we go," he said. "I'll bring some bread sticks in the meantime, to hold you." His crafty eyes glanced from Carly to me and back again. "Lemon is on the side. But don't let it make a sour face for you," he said slyly.

Carly smiled up to him. "Thank you, Sam."

Afterward we kept the conversation light. The pizza came and it was delicious, just as Sam promised.

I was ready to propose going somewhere for a few drinks, when Carly said, "I hope you don't mind too much if we call it a night, Bryan."

"It's still daytime," I said, trying to hide my disappointment.

"I know."

"He killed the day for you, didn't he, that fool David. Ruined it for all of us."

"It's not him, per se," Carly said. "I'd feel better being home with Lisa. She may not want to talk, but if she needs to, I'd like to be there to listen. Not to give advice. This isn't the time for it. She's been hurt pretty badly." Her eyes were soft on me as she spoke.

"Okay. Sounds reasonable. You want me to call you or should I wait for you to call me?"

"I'll call you."

* * * * *

The drive home was quiet, both of us lost in our private thoughts. When I pulled up to her apartment, she leaned across to me. I tilted her chin and pressed my lips gently on hers. I thought I felt a little tremor pass through her as she pulled away.

"You don't have to walk me to the door, Bryan."

"Okay," I said, watching her slide out.

"Goodnight."

"I'll wait to hear from you."

Chapter 17

When I entered our apartment I found Lisa lying face down on the bed. I gently pressed the door closed behind me, removed my shoes and padded softly across the room. Leaning over the bed, I whispered, "Lisa, are you sleeping...? Lisa...?" She didn't answer. "...Good, then sleep."

I turned to leave when I stepped on something hard on the floor beside the bed. Reaching down, I picked up an empty plastic container and read the label. It took a moment for me to realize what it was. I wheeled around. "Lisa. Lisa, wake up! Wake up!" I shook her, shook her hard and turned her over. Lisa's mouth hung open. "Lisa, wake up!"

In a panic, I flung myself across the bed, reaching for the phone on the nightstand. I cried out, "Oh God, oh, my God, Lisa! What did you do?" My frantic fingers tried to find the numbers 911.

Words jumbled and almost incoherent by panic finally got the message through. "...yes, yes, and please, hurry!"

Waiting and shivering with fright, I desperately fumbled with the phone, trying to call Bryan. Within minutes the rescue squad was there monitoring Lisa's vitals and scrambling to get her onto a stretcher and out into the ambulance. The police arrived simultaneously and questioned me. My sentences were jumbled, but I explained as best I could the circumstances that led to Lisa taking the pills. By the time Bryan arrived I was there alone.

Bryan held me in his arms calming me, soothing me with encouraging words.

"She'll be all right," he said, sitting on the bed and pulling me down next to him to hear what I already told the police. "It's a good thing you came straight home. Your woman's intuition was right on target. Don't worry, Carly. They'll take care of her at the hospital. She'll be fine."

"Oh, Bryan, I hope so," I said, clinging to his arm. "I really hope so. The poor thing and…and all because of that…that—"

"Forget him, Carly, he's not worth thinking about. As long as she's okay nothing else matters."

"Bryan, can we see her? Can we go now?"

"They probably rushed her through the back of the emergency room where we can't get to her. I'm sure they'll have to pump her stomach or do whatever it takes to bring her around and stabilize her." He rose and helped me to my feet. "But we can go over and wait."

He dabbed my eyes with a tissue. "Yes, let's. I want to see her as soon as she's conscious. I can't believe this, I just can't."

"Where did you say they took her?"

"Mercy Hospital."

"Okay, let's go."

When we arrived at the hospital we were told Lisa was being treated and hadn't been taken to a room yet, but that we'd be notified as soon as one became available. We waited in the lobby, pacing, talking for awhile, then going silent as we watched the time crawl slowly by.

Finally, three hours later we were approached by a youthful doctor who gave us the news that Lisa would be fine, and had been given a sedative.

"It's fortunate she got to us as quickly as she did," the doctor said. "It could have been much worse. Until we can contact her family, the nurse will take any necessary information you can give. She'll also provide you with instructions regarding her immediate care. Right now she's a little groggy and needs rest, so don't stay too long," he advised.

Inside room 314 Lisa was propped up in bed, her head sideways on the pillow and her eyes open. Tears started in her eyes when I walked in, followed by Bryan. She turned her head away. Her chest heaved as she tried suppressing her sobs.

Bryan touched my arm and backed out, pointing and mouthing he'd be in the waiting room.

I slid a chair alongside the bed. "It's all right, Lisa," I said, reaching over and stroking her arm. "You're fine now. Everything is going to be OK."

"I wish I was dead," Lisa said, trying to bury her head in the pillow.

"No, Lisa! Don't talk like that."

"I can't help it, Carly. That's how I feel. Everything I do seems to go wrong. Everything! I even failed trying to kill myself. My whole life is a wreck. Why couldn't you leave me alone, Carly? Why couldn't everybody leave me alone and just let me die?"

"Stop it, Lisa. It's not the end of the world. You're just upset about what happened today?"

Lisa swung around, facing me. "Yes, I'm upset about today and every day. Nothing I do goes right for me. Ever. And I'm always on the losing end. It's been that way my whole life."

"That's not true, Lisa. And today wasn't as bad as you think. A little rough in spots, I suppose, but certainly not tragic enough to call for something like this," I said, waving my hand to our surroundings. "We all have miserable days sometimes that don't go right, Lisa."

Tears streamed from the corners of her eyes. "I'm so ashamed, Carly, so ashamed. I wanted you to like David, I really did, and then... then...."

"We did, Lisa. Bryan thought he was a nice guy, rugged but nice, and so did I. Honest."

"Oh, stop it, Carly, stop it! Don't try to make me feel good. I could see your faces when he was making those stupid jokes he thought were so funny. He thought everybody thought he was a riot, but he was just making an ass out of himself. And me. Saying in front of me and you and everybody that I looked like a— oh, God!" Tears gushed from her eyes.

"Don't, Lisa, don't. Please don't be so hard on yourself. I know a couple of his remarks hurt you, but believe me, I don't even remember what they were. Neither does anybody else. I wish you'd stop dwelling on things that hurt you. What's worse, you're magnifying them and blowing them out of proportion until you can't think straight."

Lisa reached over and touched my hand. "Carly, that's not the worst of it."

"What do you mean?"

"David blames me for everything, even for that dumb Eddie peeing all over him."

"That's ridiculous." I could feel myself disliking him even more than I already did.

"All the way home he was cursing me like you can't believe. In a way I can't blame him because the zoo was my idea. If I didn't suggest it, none of this ever would have happened. On top of it, he saw me staring at the gray hair that showed. He was so humiliated. That's when he really blew his top."

"So he is a little older than you thought."

"Not necessarily, Carly. Lots of guys get prematurely gray."

Still in denial, I thought. "I suppose you're right."

"Carly?"

"Yes?"

"David thinks you're making me prejudiced against him. He said he didn't like the way you looked at him sometimes, like he was lower than dirt. He thinks you don't like him and wants me to move out."

"And...?"

"He said he'd find another apartment for me."

"And...?

She squeezed my hand. "Oh, Carly, I was really torn because I was afraid."

"That he'd hurt you? Don't worry, you can get a restraining order against him. I'll help you. That will keep him away unless he wants to go to jail."

"Oh, Carly, not just that."

"Then what, Lisa, what?"

She bit her lip, hesitating. "I...I was afraid if I didn't do what he said, he wouldn't pay me back the money he owes me."

"Oh, Lisa...you didn't."

"Over five thousand dollars."

"Lisa, Lisa."

"But I don't really care about that, Carly, not the money, really. I didn't want to move because I love you and you understand me even when I don't understand myself. You're my best friend. At the same time, I wanted to calm him down and show him I cared for him, so I didn't answer. Not right away, I guess, or fast enough, so he slapped me." Tears rolled as she spoke and turned her face sideways. "See? The mark's still there, isn't it? He slapped me hard, Lisa, very hard. He hurt me."

I felt my anger growing. "Lisa, you—"

"No, Carly, you don't have to talk me out of anything because I broke up with him. I told him never to call me again and said I could never be with a man who beats up a woman. Oh, then he really went out of control. I never saw him so angry. Look at my arms." She twisted them around. "All black and blue where he grabbed me. His face was right in front of mine and it looked so ugly, all scrunched up like that, like he wanted to kill me. I wish he would have, but I was terrified. He said I could never leave him until *he* was ready to let me go. He said he had invested too much time in me. I was crying pretty hard by then and told him okay, I'd do whatever he wanted."

"Lisa! You can't mean you're going to see him again? Not after what he did to you?"

"No, Carly, I said it so he'd get out of my car and I could get away. When he got to the curb across the street, I yelled to him not to see me or call me anymore or I'd call the police and that I didn't want anything to do with him ever again. I shouted it was final, and then I just pulled away as fast as I could. I could hardly see through the tears blinding me, but I saw him in my side-view mirror pointing his finger at me, like he was saying, 'I'll get you.'"

I looked down at her and gently smoothed her arm. "I think you made a wise decision, Lisa, I really do."

"Don't say anything, Carly, please, just don't say anything. Don't give me any sympathy or I'll just break down crying more. My eyes are burning. Let me sleep now. I'm exhausted. Totally."

"Sure," I said, bending over to hug her. "Why wouldn't you be. Get some rest now, Lisa. They should be releasing you tomorrow, probably in the afternoon. I'll check early in the morning and be here to pick you up."

Chapter 18

My phone rang as I entered my apartment.

"Hello," I said, in a melodic voice, expecting to hear Carly's voice.

"Well, don't we sound all cheerful this fine day."

I know my voice dropped an octave. "Oh, hello, Cindy."

"My, that's a quick change in the weather."

"Cindy—"

"Don't you believe in checking your messages?"

"I haven't had time."

"Haven't had time, or haven't had time for me."

"Cindy, I thought we were going to cool it for a while."

"We're not going through this again, are we, Bryan? Isn't it time we put an end to this childishness, this stupid charade?"

"It's not a charade, Cindy?"

"Well, what else would *you* call it? For three years we've been seeing each other regularly and suddenly you're unavailable. You can at least tell me you don't like me or you hate me, but don't keep stringing me along, making excuses like we have to put some space between us for a while."

"How could I hate you, Cindy? We've had too many good times together. But the fact is that we do need space— I need space. Time to sort things out. You know I never made any commitment. You didn't either."

"We didn't have to. Didn't you ever hear the expression

200

'actions speak louder than words'? Did you forget our special moments, the words you whispered in my ear? You meant them, Bryan. Every single one of them. You were serious. And so was I."

"Cindy, you talk like I was proposing to you. We just happened to hit it off at the time. Let's face it, things change. You change, I change. It's different now. I only wanted a break because things were getting too tense with us. Now I'm not sure I ever want us to be anything more than friends, good friends if possible."

She scoffed. "All right, Bryan, I get the picture. Be honest now, come clean. There's somebody else, isn't there?"

I balked. "No, there's no one else."

"There's somebody else and you don't need me anymore."

"I told you there's no one else."

"Then why are you brushing me off? I'm not asking you to marry me, you know. I only want us to get together like old times. Just once in a while like we used to. Is that asking too much?" Her voice softened. "I need you, Bryan. I miss you, honey. I miss you terribly."

"Cindy, stop. Give me time, okay? Give me time to think and maybe—"

"To think about what! So you can forget me completely and get rid of me?"

"Of course not. I—"

"Then why are you torturing me this way?"

"I'm not torturing you."

"Yes, you are and you know you are. And why are you being so mysterious? You never return my calls. You don't give me a reason except saying something stupid like you 'need space.'"

"Cut it out, Cindy. You're making a federal case out of nothing."

"Nothing! I can't sleep nights because of you. I can't concentrate at work. I'm depressed and find myself crying for no apparent reason. People keep asking me what's wrong. You're driving me crazy, Bryan, that's what's wrong, and you call it nothing?"

"Cindy—"

The line went dead. I set my phone aside and wiped the sweat from my brow. Well, maybe she'll give up now, I thought. But knowing Cindy....

Chapter 19

My phone rang again. I hesitated before answering. "What now?"

"Oops. Another cranky call?"

"Oh, Carly, sorry about that. My nerves are a little frazzled."

"You want to talk about it?"

"Another time, okay?"

"It all sounds very mysterious."

"Not really."

"If you say so."

"I say so."

"Oh, really, if *you* say so."

"I didn't mean it the way it sounded, Carly."

She laughed. "I know that. By the way, Lisa will be getting released by noon, so I'll be picking her up."

"Can you handle it or do you want me to help?"

"No, it shouldn't be a problem. I want to try talking her into seeing a counselor, but I don't think she'll be willing. Not right now, anyway."

"Give her time, Carly. She's been through some trauma. She should come around."

"We'll know soon enough. Anyway, Bryan, I don't know your schedule, but will you be available on Monday, about noon?"

"I could be, why?"

"I'm going to the Aurora library in the morning to research a paper. Since I probably won't be able to see you for at least a few days, I thought maybe we can have lunch together. I'm treating."

"In that case I'll be there."

"You know where it is?"

"On Main Street, of course."

"All right, then, it's a date. Noon, don't forget."

"I won't."

"And Bryan...?"

"Yeah...?"

"Maybe you'd better take a quick look to see who's calling before you answer..."

* * * * *

On Sunday, I spent the afternoon at my mother's house. After eating a plate of spaghetti and meat balls, we went into the living room.

"That was excellent, Mom."

"All you have to do is come back home to live."

"The offer's tempting."

Sitting in the living room across from her, I parried her questions about Carly as I tapped away at the same time on my laptop.

"So, aren't you seeing the new girl— the waitress, what's her name...?"

"Carly."

"Her, yes, Carly. Aren't you seeing her this weekend?"

"I saw her yesterday. We went to the zoo."

"The zoo. Oh, how nice, Bryan. Did you have a good time?"

"The first time I've been there in years."

"I haven't been there since your father and I took you and your brother Tommy."

"That's a lot of years ago, Mom."

"I always loved the zoo, especially going in the monkey house. The way they dash around swinging and chasing each other was so much fun to watch. I'd swear they were human, the way they would suddenly stop right in the middle of their play and stare you right in the eye."

I smiled. "Sometimes more human than you could guess, Mom."

She questioned me about Carly, where she was from, what her parents do, what her interests are—one question after the other. It made me acutely aware of how little I really knew about Carly. Of course, my mother thought I was just playing dumb, for whatever reason, and she finally gave up prying.

I decided tomorrow would be the day I'd get some answers. Enough of the game playing and secrecy. It was time to clear the air.

Chapter 20

Carly looked up from the books and papers scattered on the table in front of her. Her eyes opened wide. "Bryan," she said, glancing at her watch. "It's only 11:00. I didn't expect you till noon."

I pulled a chair up beside her, reached over and squeezed her hand.

"I was busy but I caught a break. Go ahead with what you're doing, though, don't let me interfere. Anyway, how's Lisa doing? Everything okay?"

"So far she seems to be managing. A big difference from what she was but still not where she should be. I don't know if she'll ever get over this whole thing."

"As the saying goes, 'Time heals all.'" I slid in closer. "I hope I'm not in the way."

"No problem. I only wish I didn't have to spend the whole day here working on this paper." She picked up a page. "How does my topic sound: 'The Effects of Malnutrition on Early Educational Development'?"

"Sounds like a book of recipes."

"Bryan, seriously."

"Sounds good to me. But look," I said, standing up, "you keep working and I'll browse around the book shelves for the next hour until you're ready."

"You sure you don't mind, just browsing?"

"No, really, I do it a lot. It's one of my favorite pastimes. Browsing, that is, not carousing. Although if I was looking at cars at a dealership, I suppose you might call that car-ousing."

Her lips twisted into a wry smile. "Personally, I think you spent a little too much time with David."

I left her there and started down one of the fiction aisles. I marveled at the books, row upon row, dozens, hundreds, thousands of them, each one the product of someone's imagination. Anyone of them might have taken a year, two years or ten years to write. It boggled the mind to think of how many centuries of concentrated thought were captured here between covers since *Gilgamesh, the Bible, the Iliad.*

I plucked out a copy of Dickens' *Great Expectations* and hefted it in my hand. I read the book in high school and remembered the main character, Pip, and his sister's husband Joe. They were so real I could still envision them and others, like Estella and Orlick; yet all those people were fictional, born in Dickens' head and, like other fictional characters, created to populate the world of books.

My mind took a funny turn, and I imagined the library as the cosmos, and the characters suddenly breaking from the story line and talking to each other about their own being, of how they got there, what they were doing there, and the possible existence of a god. Unable to see beyond their universe of pages, they would have no way to prove they had a Creator. And because they couldn't explain their presence, they couldn't disprove it either. Some would argue there is no god. Others would argue there must be a god, and that those living a good life would be reincarnated, a sequel, if you will....

Well, Dickens is certainly dead, I thought, but his creations live on. And for us, the living, maybe God *is* dead, as Nietzsche said, or perhaps he's an absentee Landlord who left us a conundrum of paradoxes from which his tenants may infer the fact of his existence.

I wandered into the sections on history, philosophy—wherever my nose led me—science, picking up a tome here and there. Many, I knew, represented a lifetime of work. I pondered the idea. To think, someone had spent his life exploring and studying a subject, and any one of us could take his book and, in the space of a week or so, have the benefit of all the years of his accumulated knowledge and experience. We could hold in our hands the words and thoughts of the greatest minds that ever lived: Plato, St. Augustine, Shakespeare, Descartes, Hume and so many others. We could read and absorb their ideas and wisdom and make them our own. Anyone could gather thousands of years of human experience and knowledge in the short span of a single lifetime. It didn't seem possible we could be anything but geniuses with all that knowledge at our fingertips.

I passed the shelves stacked from top to bottom, looking at the titles, so many books, so enticing, all wanting to be read. I felt hopelessly overwhelmed. They seemed to cry out with silent voices, 'Read me, please, read me.'

I thought it would make a good fantasy story, one set in a library after closing time, when the characters would call out and argue among themselves, have a war of ideas, seeking to understand their relationships and their place in their musty universe. It could be even more interesting if the deceased authors, calling themselves Creators, would step out of their biographies to challenge the statements of their characters, and open a new speculative dialogue on First Causes.

After an hour of browsing and musing, I ambled back to Carly's table.

"I'm all set," she said.

"Hungry?"

"Yes, definitely."

"There's a restaurant a couple of doors away."

"Good," she said, shuffling papers together. "Did you discover anything new?"

"Only that God may be a librarian."

She frowned.

"And it's possible we're just words on a page, just that and nothing more."

"Is there a joke in there someplace I'm not getting?"

"If there is, it may be on us."

"Okay," she said, stacking a little pile, "let me put it a simpler way: Did you find any interesting books to take out?"

"Yes, all of them."

She smiled up with bright blue eyes. "I know the feeling."

"And the feeling here," I said, rubbing the back of my sore neck.

"I know exactly what you mean." She slid her books into the large bag beside her.

"It might be a good idea if the library books were stacked flat on vertically rotating shelves, or were at least built on an angle so you wouldn't have to cock your head reading titles until your neck's paralyzed…. Hey, how's that for a cartoon," he said. "Show a line of people going up the stairs into a library, heads straight, and a line of people coming out, all with their heads cocked to the side." He chuckled. "If Lisa's boyfriend David was here, he might even suggest selling the idea to a chiropractor for an advertisement."

"I'm so glad she's finally rid of that beast."

"Personally, I think the guy's more than a little off his

rocker."

"Ready?"

We talked as she checked out a few books before continuing our way through the corridor and down the stairs to the outside. We barely made the parking lot when a voice called out:

"Bryan! Bryan Perri!" She rushed up to me and threw her arms around me. "How are you, sweetie?"

"Cindy," I said, startled.

"Oh, don't answer, just kiss me," she cooed, pressing her lips to mine.

I tried to free myself. "Wait—"

"I haven't heard from you in days, honey. You said you'd call last weekend," she said, backing off looking hurt and holding me at arm's length. "I waited and waited. Did something happen you want to tell me about?"

Flustered, I looked to Carly, who stood frozen in place.

Cindy pulled me in and wrapped her arms tight around me. "I was so worried I even drove over to your apartment, but you weren't there."

"Cindy. I...I—"

"How could you forget our anniversary, sweetie?" she said, sliding her hands up around my neck.

"Cindy, this is...." I turned, but Carly had already spun on her heel and was striding toward her car. "Carly," I called after her. "Carly, wait!"

"I know who she is," Cindy said, pushing me away angrily. "And I know she's the reason I haven't heard from you."

"Carly," I called again, "wait, I can explain!" Embarrassed

and angry at myself, I turned back to Cindy. "What the hell is this all about? What is it with this ambush? And what do you mean 'our anniversary'?"

"Why, sweetie, three years ago today, remember? When we met?"

"I thought we had an understanding."

"You did, not me. You can't just toss me aside like a used rag, not Cindy Megan! I knew there was another girl. I could feel it in my bones."

"Have you been following me around, spying on me?"

"Why, sweetie, what's the matter, guilty conscience?"

"Look, Cindy, where I go and who I see is none of your business."

"Really? You mean no one can know you're seeing Carly Miller, daughter of the once prominent Edward Edmond Miller?"

I guess I looked as stunned as I felt.

"Oh, hasn't she told you the sad story about her unhappy family? How near bankruptcy they are? Look it up. Maybe she isn't as close to you as you thought?"

"What she told me or didn't tell me is none of your business."

"Maybe she isn't, but you are."

I looked anxiously down the aisle, where I saw Carly's car swerving around a stop sign and into the street.

"Get out of my life, Cindy," I shouted as I moved away. I don't want to see you again. You're vicious and vindictive. And don't call me anymore. Ever!"

"You can't just drop me, Bryan!" she called after me. "I've been good to you. I've been loyal and loving. You can't just toss me aside like an old shoe. I've given too much of my life to you." She shook her finger at me. "I'm warning you...you...!"

I could still hear her ranting as I raced over to my car, climbed in and shot out of the lot into the street. But I was too late. Carly was long gone and already out of sight. I slapped the wheel. "Damn you, Cindy Megan, you damn troublemaker. Damn you!"

Chapter 21

I spent the next few miserable days reliving the event at the library. Cindy did a good job of sabotaging my relationship with Carly, and she did it purely out of spite, out of unadulterated malice. Cindy knew as well as I did that it was all over between us, but her vindictive nature wouldn't let me off easy. She's probably still gloating, I thought, knowing the damage she inflicted on me. I called Carly several times since then, hoping to pacify her, but each time it was the same story. I tried again:

"Hi, Lisa. This is Bryan. "How are you feeling?"

"I'm fine, thank you."

"Good to hear that, Lisa. Is Carly there?"

"I'm sorry, she's not."

"Is she working?"

"I really couldn't say. She could have a class."

"Do you know when she'll be back?"

"No, I don't know."

"I don't know if she'll answer her phone if I call her. Will you tell her to call me when she gets home? Maybe that'll work."

"Okay."

I knew Lisa was lying. Her flat, unfriendly tone told me Carly had confided in her about what happened and, naturally, being close friends, Lisa sympathized with her completely. They'd become true soul mates now. Both believed they were betrayed by men they trusted. Carly must have told her to brush me off if he called, and Lisa was only too happy to oblige. All I could do now was try to catch Carly on the job and hope to straighten things out.

* * * * *

The Four Seasons restaurant greeted me with the strong smell of coffee and soft music when I came in early that evening. I took in at a glance the few customers scattered around as I headed for a booth offering a strategic view of the place. Behind the counter a waitress busied herself stacking dishes. Moments later another emerged from the back room, picked up a menu and hurried over to me. She slowed when she saw me.

"Hello, Lisa."

"Hello," she said, avoiding my eyes and handing me the menu.

"I don't need it. I'll have coffee… and a cheeseburger."

"How do you want it done?"

"Medium. Nothing on it but ketchup."

"It's right there," she said, indicating the ketchup bottle on the table with her pencil and jotting down the order. "Is that it?"

"Yes, except…is Carly on tonight?"

"No," she said, snatching back the menu and leaving before I could ask when I might catch her there.

I ate slowly, brooding. I had just finished my sandwich and was reaching for my money, when I spotted the familiar face of David, Lisa's lover-boyfriend, come through the door. Head low, he took off his hat and set it on the seat beside him in a booth farther down. His back was to me.

214

I didn't like the feel of things. I'd already heard enough from Carly to know the guy was trouble or, in mealy-mouth modern day parlance, had 'issues.' I decided to hang around to see if anything developed.

I didn't have to wait long.

I could see Lisa's face turn pale as she approached David's booth and saw him sitting there. Their voices were quiet enough when she leaned in and took his order. For a few moments I thought everything might be all right as he watched her leave and return with his coffee. She glanced around furtively, apparently forgetting, or not caring, about my presence, and sat down beside David. Even though rap music was playing in the background, I could hear the tension in their rising and falling voices.

Several patrons wandered in and filled in several booths.

The manager, another waitress, blowing a wisp of yellow peroxide hair off her forehead, called out to her. "Lisa."

Lisa slid out and stood up. From where I sat, I could see David's hand shoot out and grab her wrist. She tried to pull herself free.

"David," she said, looking around, "please!"

His voice rose. "Please, my ass. Sit down. I'm not finished with you."

"Let go," she whispered hoarsely. "People are watching."

"Fuck 'em. I'm talking to you."

"Not now, David, please. I'll meet you later."

"Now."

"You're going to make me lose my job."

"Too goddamned bad. Sit down!"

She struggled against him. "David, please!"

David slid out and stood up beside her. "Get your coat."

"Are you crazy?"

"You're coming with me, and you're coming now!"

"David, please let me go, please." She tried to pull herself away.

David's hand came down across her face with a loud slap.

Cowering, Lisa screamed.

I was about to jump out and help her when suddenly a young guy with blonde hair and a baby face leaped out of the corner booth and dove between the two of them. David's fist came down on him like a hammer, dropping the boy to the floor, but he bounced up again and lunged for David.

Having broken free, Lisa ran toward the kitchen screaming for the manager to call 911.

The boy wrapped his arm around David's neck, but couldn't hold on when David swiveled and slammed him over the table in the booth where he jack-hammered punch after punch into his face. His mouth and nose bloody, the boy kicked himself free of David and sprang at him again, determined and relentless, fighting as if his life were at stake.

It was then that I saw the glint of a knife in David's hand, saw it high in the air and lost sight of it as it plunged into the boy's body. The boy's arms flailed against the blade flashing down in a series of quick strokes.

Along with another guy who'd been sitting at the counter, I leaped up and together we jumped David. David collapsed under the weight of the two of us on his back and clawed at my arms encircling his neck. He bellowed as a third guy jumped in and stomped on David's hand, freeing the bloody knife and kicking it away.

With David cursing and struggling mightily, the three of us pinned him down tight until the police finally arrived and took over, cuffing him on the floor and hauling him to his feet.

"You fat whore," he cried out to Lisa, rage burning his eyes, and resisting the two cops as they jacked him out through the door toward their waiting car. "I'm not finished with you yet, you bitch," he screamed over his shoulder, "not by a long shot!" He continued screaming threats until his words were lost in the dying sound of a siren pulling into the parking lot.

Moments later the paramedics came rushing in to help the boy on the floor, while everyone else backed away.

One threw a cuff around his arm to check his blood pressure while another worked quickly to stanch the bleeding from the various wounds. When they were finished, they loaded him onto a stretcher and hurried out the door with him to the ambulance. In the meantime three more patrol cars had rolled up with police who had come and in were taking statements from witnesses.

Before giving my own statement, I asked one of the paramedics where they were taking the boy. I was putting on my jacket and about to leave, when Lisa approached, her eyes still tearing.

"Bryan, I'm sorry," she said, visibly shaking. "Carly's home. Could you stop there and explain to her what happened before I get there? I can't make myself do it. Carly was right," she said, her words choking her. "I promised I would never speak to him or look at him again if I ever saw him."

"I think it can wait, Lisa. I want to go to the hospital now to see how this young guy makes out. It's been about an hour already. But I can make a phone call on the way if it's okay with you."

"Oh, please, then let me go with you. I have to thank him personally, I really do. I hope he's okay. If it hadn't been for him—"

"I think his injuries looked worse than they were, at least that's the impression the paramedic gave me... Okay, get your coat."

Rushing into the kitchen area, she called over to her manager. "Martha, I'm sorry. I have to leave."

"Don't worry about it, honey, I understand. I already called Janice to cover for you. We'll manage till she gets here."

Chapter 22

When we arrived at the hospital, the ER was jammed with people waiting for treatment, several with casts on their arms, others with bandaged hands and faces, and others with less obvious problems, but with faces showing pain.

"I don't see him," Lisa said.

"That's because these are walk-ins. When an ambulance brings anyone in, they're priority and go straight back to a room for treatment." I was going to mention it was the same way when she was brought in, but decided not to open that still-fresh wound. "Wait here a minute," I said.

Poring over paperwork, the triage nurse didn't look up when she asked what she could do for me. I flashed my ID and said I was an attorney inquiring after the young man brought in a little earlier with stab wounds.

"His name is..." she said, glancing at my wallet and checking her chart "...Contini, Robert Contini."

"Yes," I said, "that's him."

She moved the mouse around on her computer, looked up and said, "He's out of surgery. They're getting a room ready for him at the moment."

Contini. Could it be? I thought, going back to Lisa, where she found a seat in the corner.

"What did you find out?" she asked, anxiously.

"Apparently he's okay. They're just waiting to get him into a room."

"That sounds encouraging."

"I take it as a positive sign, too. If he was really bad he'd still be in surgery or ICU or they wouldn't say anything at all."

"Oh, God, how could this happen?" she said, holding her head. "It's all so crazy, like a bad dream, a terrible nightmare."

"I'll give Carly another try now and see if she's home yet. I have to go outside to use this," I said, nodding toward the sign on the wall prohibiting cell phones, and whipping out my phone. "Anything special you want me to tell her?"

"Tell her to come here. I'd like her to be with me. I need her for moral support."

"Let's hope she takes my call."

"Oh, Bryan, I'm sorry, I'm honestly very sorry. If she doesn't, let me talk."

I stepped outside on the sidewalk and tapped in the number. She answered on the second ring.

"Wait, wait, Carly," I shouted, "don't hang up. I'm at the hospital with Lisa."

"Lisa! Again? Is she hurt?"

"No, she's fine, believe me, she's fine. Why don't you come down here and I'll explain everything— or Lisa will, if you like."

"Where? What hospital?"

"Where we were last time, Mercy Hospital. Right now we're in the ER...."

I went back inside and stood next to Lisa. "She's on her way down."

"I'm so glad." She glanced around and lowered her voice to a near whisper. "Bryan, I hope you can work things out with Carly. I'm sure there must be some explanation, but she is really hurt."

"I know."

"Strictly between us, Bryan, I know she cares for you."

I looked at her doubtfully. "You know?"

"We've been friends a long time. I've seen how she acts with other guys who wanted to date her. No matter how nice they seemed or how handsome they were— and it didn't make any difference if they had money or were important or not— they never lasted long. She can't hide her feelings from me, not for long anyway, and I know she loves you. This latest trouble couldn't change that. I can't prove it, but I just know it."

My heart leaped with joy at her words, even though, sad as it was, I saw several people literally stagger in holding their stomachs or bleeding heads.

Fifteen minutes later an elderly couple entered, a matronly woman holding a handkerchief to her eyes. The slouch-shouldered man beside her hobbled in, with the woman's arm locked in his. When they approached the desk, I recognized him before I heard his inquiry.

I waited until he turned away from the nurse. "Sam," I said, walking over to him.

Sam didn't recognize me immediately in this different environment. "Who?"

"Sam, it's me, Bryan."

"Who Bryan?"

"In your restaurant, remember? Bryan and Carly, like Carly Simon, the singer."

Sam's eyes opened wide in amazement. "Bryan. Sure." He turned to his wife. "Caterina, the love birds. In our restaurant."

He glanced around.

"Carly's on her way now," I said. Then, "You're here for your grandson."

"Yes, Bobby. How…how did you know?"

"I was there when it happened."

"Caterina, you hear? Our Bobby. Bryan, he was there."

Mrs. Contini looked up, nodding and still dabbing at her eyes. "I heard."

"He's out of surgery, the nurse just told me. He'sa okay. Gonna be like new. They're gonna find a room for him any minute."

"That's good news."

"And you, you, Bryan? You got a problem to be here, too?"

"No, I wanted to come down to see how your Bobby made out. I didn't know he was your grandson until I heard the name."

"My God, Caterina, you hear that? It's like a miracle. It's like—"

At that moment Carly came through the door and Lisa jumped up to greet her. Carly hugged her. "Lisa, what happened? Are you all right?"

"Carly, you won't believe it, you just won't. It was all so horrible and happened so fast." She pointed. "Bryan's over there, talking to that old couple."

Carly's eyes opened wide when she spotted me waving her over to them.

"Bryan," she said, a cool note in her voice. "Sam! Oh, my gosh," she said, stepping over with Lisa tagging behind and giving Sam a hug.

"Caterina, this is Carly, like I told you before. In the lovers' booth."

"I know, I know," she said, nodding her head again and again. "You said it already. I got ears. How many times you gonna tell me. I can hear. You don't have to keep telling me, I know…How do you do, Carly?"

Carly looked from face to face. "I don't understand."

"Carly," Lisa said, "the guy in the restaurant, remember? You know who I mean. The one that always sits in my section?"

Carly looked puzzled for a moment. "The guy with the marbles…or the one with the sweater?"

"No, not marble-mouth. Him, the one with the sweater. Well, David came in like everything was normal and he just wanted to talk, and when I wouldn't leave with him he went crazy and tried dragging me and beating up on me."

"Oh, Lisa!"

"He didn't hurt me though, except my wrist, but he would have if not for the guy jumping in and saving me."

I took over from there, explaining the circumstances to Carly as well as to Sam and his wife.

"Your grandson's a hero, Sam… Mrs. Contini."

"You hear that, Caterina, our Bobby's a hero."

"I know, I know," she said, bobbing her head, "I got ears, too."

"And the nurse, she said she talked to the doctor, and he'sa all done surgery. Gonna be okay. He'sa gonna be here a coupla days, joosta to make sure. Then he'sa coming home."

We stayed together awhile rehashing the details until Sam and his wife left to go to their grandson's room.

Before I left, I managed to catch the surgeon leaving the doctors' lounge. He was a portly, middle-aged man with a bushy mustache:

"He's a lucky kid," the doctor said, putting on his green cap and adjusting his stethoscope.

"I know he took quite a few cuts. It looked pretty bad to me, seeing him on the floor like he was."

"The blood would make it look that way, but most of his wounds were superficial, except for the one near his heart. That one was very serious. Another inch and—" He made a face...

* * * * *

I stood in the hospital parking lot talking to Carly and Lisa. "Lisa, if you want a ride back to the restaurant or home, I'll take you."

Carly spoke up. Her voice chilly. "I'll take her," she said.

"Fine." I hesitated, not sure if I wanted to say anything in front of Lisa. After a moment's thought, I figured I had no choice and nothing to lose. "Carly, will you let me take you out— to a restaurant or someplace— and give me a chance to explain about the other day? An hour, half an hour—"

Carly's lips were tight. "I don't think so, Bryan. There's nothing to explain. I—"

"Oh, Carly, for cripe's sake," Lisa interrupted, "at least give the guy a chance to tell his side of the story."

Carly shot her a fiery look. "How can I believe *anything* he says? I didn't find out until a few minutes ago that he's a lawyer. If it wasn't for the nurse talking in there, I still wouldn't know."

I took her arm. "Carly, I tried to tell you, but when you let me know you didn't hold lawyers in very high regard, well, I didn't want to take the chance, not yet, not until you got to know me better."

"You were right first time in Sam's when you told me the truth isn't always there on the surface to be seen. I should have known you were hiding something then."

"Carly, excuse me if I'm wrong, but I wonder, is there anything you've been hiding from me? Something maybe you should have told *me* about?"

Lisa broke in again. "Carly, for once in your life stop being so stubborn. Tell him you'll meet him so I don't have to stand here and be subjected to all this…this stuff."

Carly bit down on her lip.

"Or," Lisa continued, "if for no other reason, Carly, do if for me. Bryan helped, you know. If it wasn't for him jumping in you might be looking for a new roommate."

Carly pulled herself up straight. "All right, Bryan. Tell me when and where you want to meet."

"That's all I'm asking, Carly. Just a little time to explain. An hour at most."

Her manner was icy. "All right. Not that it will do either of us any good, I'm sure."

"I'll call you in a couple of days, if it's okay with you."

We parted ways there, and I watched them go, their arms around each other. I walked over to my car, still watching, but Carly never looked back, never even snuck a glance. Not even once.

Chapter 23

I went through the next few days haunted by the memory of Carly at the hospital. I'd never seen her so cold, so determined to break it off between us. If it hadn't been for Lisa butting in and saying what she did, I doubted she'd have agreed to see me again— ever. Still, it wasn't easy for me to surrender my pride and have someone plead my case, like I was a pathetic victim begging for mercy. I only allowed it because I knew she was acting on a lie she thought was the truth, and I wasn't about to lose her on that account. I couldn't let a misunderstanding ruin our relationship. And I would never give Cindy the satisfaction of making it happen.

Carly made it sound as if I was keeping a whole secret life from her by not mentioning I was a lawyer. And of course with Cindy throwing a bomb between us the way she did, well, that's all she needed to break off our relationship.

But if there was more to me, there was more to her, too. A lot more. Cindy mentioned that Carly was the daughter of Edward Edmond Miller, a well-known industrialist who'd apparently fallen on hard times. Carly never told me anything about it, or anything else at all about her past, for that matter. What else was she holding back? Was she perhaps jilted by someone she'd been deeply in love with, and that's why Cindy's appearance had such a devastating effect on her? I bet myself I was close to the truth on that.

Over the next few days I researched Carly's family background. I had thought of doing it before but resisted because I felt a guilty sense of invading her privacy. Now she left me no choice.

I found Carly Miller's family was originally the Mueller

family, who had left Germany in 1763 and established themselves in a small, northern Pennsylvania town. The patriarch, Frederick Mueller, along with his younger brother Otto, began first with a feed business and later established a small brewery. Within a few years they became leading businessmen in the community. Always looking for new opportunities, Frederick turned to producing fabrics for uniforms, saddle blankets and other military items during the Revolutionary War, which very soon made him a rich man.

After the building of the Erie Canal across New York State in 1825, Frederick's son Maximilian moved the family and operations north to the Buffalo area and opened a small textile factory, which held its own against bigger companies until the outbreak of the Civil War, when great- grandson Karl Mueller expanded operations and became one of the biggest suppliers of military equipment to the Union army.

The company, renamed Miller Industries, went public in 1923 and continued to grow well into the 20th Century. Business temporarily flagged during the Great Depression of the 1930s, but only in recent years, particularly since the NAFTA Agreements, did its fortunes begin a steady and irreversible decline. Labor problems and competition from overseas, particularly the Asian countries, cut deep inroads into the company's profits, causing major contractions in its business operations nationally and internationally. With the value of its stock plummeting in recent years, the present CEO and president, Edward Edmond Miller, has been seeking ways to restructure the company and avoid insolvency.

I was bogged down with court appearances and didn't get back to Carly for several days. I had even tussled with myself trying to decide if it was even worth another attempt to get together again. If I knew these rich people as well as I thought I did, it was possible that Carly's family would threaten to

228

disown her if she married "below her class." Whatever the reason, Carly now seemed so dead-set against me, I felt my cause was hopeless and I'd only make a fool of myself. How could I convince her I hadn't been seeing Cindy; it would take a miracle. Cindy's dramatic performance was so damned powerful, especially with the details: calling me 'honey,' her talk about seeing me on the weekend and our 'anniversary.' And the intimacy of that kiss! Who wouldn't fall for that well-planned scheme? Could I possibly blame Carly for distrusting me, for not wanting to have anything to do with me, for dumping me?

What the hell do I have to lose? I asked myself. She's just as much gone now as she ever will be. But if we talk, at least I'd have a chance. Maybe only one in a million, but still a chance. As it stands.... I decided to call.

I was about to call Carly when my phone rang.

"It's me, sweetie. I hope you're not mad."

"Mad?" I scoffed. "Mad doesn't begin to express what I feel."

"I'm sorry, honey. I couldn't help myself."

"Well, neither can I. I told you it was over, Cindy, and it's over. You made sure of it with your fine theatrical performance. Get it through your head once and for all, it's over, o-v-e-r. If there was a shred of a chance it wasn't, you made sure it is."

"You don't mean it, honey, I know you don't."

"I don't?" I sighed with frustration. "Pulling that stunt was outrageous and the last straw. You humiliated me and you humiliated someone who doesn't deserve that kind of treatment. I don't want to have anything to do with you ever again. Understand? Ever, ever, ever again!"

"Why, Bryan, because I caught you in a lie! Telling me you

only wanted a breather and all the while you were making out with that...that thing."

"I wasn't lying about taking a time-out. Not at first. And I wasn't making out."

"Well, if you weren't, why are you so upset? It sounds like I hit a raw nerve."

"First of all because you spied on me and followed me. That's stalking. And because you barged in where you don't belong. And she's not a *thing,* as you called her."

"You've got a lot of damned nerve, Bryan. First you lie to me, then string me along making me think we'll be getting together again— saying you only wanted some space for a month or so— then you make it look as if I'm to blame for this whole damn fiasco. Well, I've got news for you. I've been true to you, waiting for us to get together the way we were meant to be, and all the while you've been out having a good time with some poor little rich bitch. I'm the injured party, Bryan, me, not you!" She started crying.

"Listen, Cindy, tears won't help. I'm calling it quits, once and for all. Chalk it up to life. Things just didn't work out for us. At one time—"

"Sure, after you used me up like an old whore, you don't need me anymore."

"Cindy, I didn't use you."

"No? Well, what do *you* call it? But it's okay, honey," she pleaded, "believe me, no hard feelings. I won't hold a grudge. Honest, I promise. Let's just say we hit a bump in the road. It happens to lots of people, maybe everybody. We can smooth this out and let bygones be bygones. Bryan, I love you. You know that. I've always loved you and I want you. We can't just throw it all away, all the good times we had together, going to the movies, the concerts, our walks along the river, making love. We can work this out; I know we can if we just give ourselves a chance. All I'm asking for is a chance, please, one chance to put this ridiculous, silly thing behind us. After all the days and months and years, yes, Bryan, years that we spent together, we owe that much to each other, don't we? I'm willing to forgive and forget."

"It's no use, Cindy. It's over. That's final. And I'd appreciate if you didn't call me anymore."

"You bastard, Bryan, you bastard! Why don't you just stick a knife in my heart, carve it out and spit on it. Get it over with Bryan. Kill me, why don't you! Just kill me!"

"Don't take it that way, Cindy. We're adults. Some things are just not meant to be."

"You can't be so cruel, Bryan. You can't! You're better than that. I invested too much of my heart and soul in us. I believed we'd be getting married someday. I never said it outright, but I believed it. I wanted your baby. Our baby."

"Cindy, no. No no no no no!"

"You can't do this to me, Bryan. I won't let you. It isn't fair. I love you."

"Accept it, Cindy. I mean it and—"

"I hate you, Bryan! I hate you, hate you hate you hate you, you rotten, heartless thing! I won't forget this. You can't do this to me. You can't ruin my life this way. I won't let you!"

"Cindy—"

The line went dead.

Taking a few deep breaths, and with a shaking hand, I tapped in Carly's number. She answered.

"Carly, will tomorrow evening be convenient for you?"

"Where at?" Her voice was neutral.

"How about where you work?"

"Why not Sam's?"

"Fine with me. What time's best for you?"

"Six-thirty?"

"Good enough. Do you want me to pick you up?"

"I'll meet you there."

After we hung up, I wondered why she chose Sam's place. To show we'd come full circle, ending where it began? She might have chosen Forest Lawn cemetery. Maybe she wanted to ask about Sam's grandson, Bobby, to see how he was doing. But she could do that any time. I didn't feel encouraged one bit. Her voice was flat throughout our brief conversation. It almost sounded to me like a business call. Well, everything was out of my hands. She had total control and I was at her mercy. I really wasn't anxious for the meeting, but I did long to see her face again. At least once more.

Chapter 24

I pulled into Sam's parking lot and found a slot next to Carly's car parked alongside the building. I climbed out and ran my hand across the hood of her car as I passed it. Heat still emanating from the radiator told me she hadn't been there too long.

When I stepped inside the building, the warmth hit me in the face and the sweet aroma of sauce and baked bread hit me in the stomach. Half the place was filled with people talking, sipping wine and bent over their plates, eating. Sam's music played softly in the background from hidden speakers.

I spotted Carly in their corner booth and made my way over to it. She was sitting, stoically it seemed to me, with her hands in her lap and a cup of coffee before her. She didn't look up till the last moment.

"Hello, Carly," I said, sliding into the booth across from her and noticing that her coffee was half gone.

"Hello, Bryan."

She still had her coat on, which told me she didn't intend to stay long. "Are you ordering anything to eat?"

"I'm not hungry."

Sam swept up at that moment. "Well, my young friend Bryan, we meet again, only this time, without so much to worry about, eh?" He looked doubtfully from face to face.

"Right, Sam. How's your grandson doing?"

"Shake-a-speare? Joosta minute ago I told Carly, he'sa fine, almost like new. She can tell you. Can I get you something now?"

"I'll have a cup of coffee, Sam, if you're not too busy."

"Sure. For you, Bryan, anything, anything at all," he said. "You too, Carly, a fresh cup. Free, on the house. I heard everything, Bryan, how you helpa our Bobby. Thank you, from the bottom of my heart. My Caterina, she thanks you, too."

"I really didn't do much, Sam. Bobby did it all. He saved the girl's life."

"Still, you helped. Don't say no...I get your coffee now," he said, moving away.

I turned my attention on Carly. With her nose slightly tilted up, she looked aloof, almost defiant and ready to hold her ground against anything I might say. "So his grandson's okay?" I asked.

"Sam said he came home last night, but I already knew it. And he was pleased to hear how Lisa spent so much time in the hospital with him."

"Lisa probably figures she owes him her life," I said.

"There's a little more there than meets the eye, as they say."

I looked at her quizzically. "More than what?"

"Well, Robbie—that's what he likes to be called— he's been a regular at the restaurant for quite a while, and he's had his eye on Lisa. She never gave him a tumble, though. She thought he was a lot younger than her because of his baby face, but it turns out he's about the same age. Anyway, for some strange reason she felt hostile toward him and after a while she wouldn't even wait on him."

"For no reason?"

"No logical reason that I could make out. It's just a peculiar thing that sometimes happens in life, I guess."

"Well, who can understand the human heart," I said, implying more than I was saying.

If Carly picked up on it, she didn't let on. "I guess the latest incident with David made her see the light."

"She hasn't been to work since it happened."

"Isn't she feeling well?" I asked. "Is she depressed?"

"Not that, no. She was spending all that time in the hospital with him, with Robbie."

"She's sure showing a lot of gratitude."

"She stayed until last night and only came home to shower and sleep."

"Heartwarming, to say the least."

Apparently forgetting herself, Carly smiled. "He even wrote a poem for her. I read it, and it's really good. It's called *Angel Descending*. Lisa's thrilled. David made a big difference in her life, but not the kind or the way she ever expected. Fate works in strange ways, I guess."

Sam returned with our coffee. "Carly told you, eh, about Bobby?"

"Yes, she did, Sam. I'm glad all is well again."

"Well?" Sam said. "Even better. I remember what Carly said to me before, the first time here, remember? About my dream. I think now I can see better. I had my dream and didn't take it. Now I'm part of Caterina's dream, so it's okay with me. For Bobby, he has his dream. Maybe he'll starve being a poet, but if 'at'sa his dream, eh, what can I say. Like I said before, you wanna guarantee, go to Target or Wal-Mart, they give it. But not when you chase a dream. 'At'sa real life."

"You'll see, Sam," I said. "He'll probably end up with a

teaching job at the university. But he won't stop writing his poetry. In time he'll publish a book of poems with his name on it. Maybe a lot of books. He'll have his cake and eat it, too."

"Hey, pretty good. Have his cake and eat it, too. That way he'sa got a dream but won't starve." He held his belly, laughing. He looked to our faces before starting away. "If you want anything more justa you let me know."

I turned back to Carly, who had tightened up again. "About the other day—"

"You don't have to explain, Bryan. It's not necessary. I—"

A record began playing:

You made me love you,

I didn't want to do it,

I didn't want to do it,

You made me want....

We both stopped talking for moment, as if someone outside ourselves was speaking for us.

"Harry James," I said.

"He's dead," she said, "And so is this relationship." She pushed her cup away.

"You're not even going to give me a chance to—"

"To explain? There's nothing to explain, Bryan. Everything's very clear. I think it's best if we part here and now."

I stared at her. "It was nice while it lasted, is that what you're telling me?"

"Phrase it however you like." She dug into her purse for her money.

I reached across and caught her hand. "Carly, don't."

"Please," she said, her eyes misty.

"Can't we talk?"

"It's no use, Bryan, don't you understand? It's not you. It's not just what happened at the library, it's— oh, what difference does it make? What difference does anything make?"

"Maybe it does. Try me."

"No. I'm asking you, don't call me anymore, please. I never should have let it go this far," she said, sliding over and standing up. "I should have known better and listened to my instincts."

"Is it your parents?" I asked. "Something to do with them?"

She looked at me curiously. "My parents have nothing to do with my decisions."

I stood up with her. "Carly."

She turned and began walking out.

"So long, you two lovebirds," Sam called from the pass-through window in the kitchen. "Come back soon."

I searched for my money, dropped a ten dollar bill on the table and hurried out after her.

She was nearly to her car when I caught up to her, took her by the arm and spun her around toward me. "Carly, this is crazy. I love you. I think you love me too. I know you do. We can't break up like this, for no good reason, we just can't."

She gazed into my eyes, her tears smudging her mascara. "We have to, Brian. I have to."

"But why, Carly, why?"

She looked away. "It won't work," she said, her voice breaking. "Don't you understand?"

"No, I don't. I want an explan—"

"Bryan!" she screamed, shoving me away at the same time a car, its wheels squealing, careened through the lot, brushing me hard enough to knock me to the ground and narrowly missing her.

Sprawled on my chest, I caught sight of the red Lexus burning rubber and smoking over the blacktop as it gunned out onto the street and sped off out of sight.

Cindy! She tried to kill me!

Stunned, nearly hysterical, Carly dropped down beside me, shaking…

Chapter 25

Kneeling beside Bryan, I remembered that awful night a half dozen years earlier… a perfect day for a wedding. I stood looking in the mirror as my mother and my best friend, Clarisse, adjusted the sleeves, pulling and tugging at the hems and folds of my white Chantilly lace gown. We giggled and gossiped between ourselves, admiring the beauty of its design and me, the bride-to-be.

But I didn't feel beautiful. My blue eyes lacked the luster and shine this special day should have put there. Within an hour I'd be married to Bertram, handsome Bertram, wonderful Bertram, wealthy Bertram Kirby III, admired by everyone as a rising executive star, heir to the Wilson-Kirby fortune and sought after by all the beautiful and available debutantes in town. So why didn't my heart go singing? Why wasn't I deliriously happy?

I remembered the church flooded with organ music, my bouquet of pink, white, and red roses, the pews crowded with admiring faces as I passed down the aisle, my six-foot train flowing behind; holding my father's arm; the solemn Reverend Troidle standing before me and Bertram, flanked by our wedding party; the sparkling blue-white diamond ring sliding on my finger; my going numb and feeling faint as I heard the final words: 'I now pronounce you husband and wife.'

All was a blur after that: the well-wishers hugging me and kissing my cheek; cameras flashing; filming by the exclusive Excelsior Studios with formally posed still shots for the family album and the newspaper's society page. And later that evening the reception at the Marriott Hotel, the whole third floor mezzanine ours, with stations spaced every fifty feet serving beverages and chocolate-covered strawberries half again the size of golf balls, platters of hors d'oeuvres of stuffed mushrooms, oysters, shrimp and cheeses among a staggering variety of delicacies to please the fussiest and most discriminating of palates; the sit-down dinner at tables decorated with bouquets of flowers, accommodating six hundred guests, with a choice of dinner ranging from lobster tails to filet mignon to partridge under glass, and desserts of baked Alaska, cherries jubilee, bananas foster or a choice of several others.

Guests laughed as they delicately clinked spoons against their glasses, coaxing us to exchange kisses; they clapped when my dad and I danced briefly before Bertram and I danced the wedding waltz to the sedate music of an eight-piece orchestra. Everyone was so happy and in such a wonderful mood. So why wasn't I? At this glorious moment in time, this vital juncture in my life, married to a wonderful man, our prospects for the future bright and so full of promise— so why did I feel discontented...unfulfilled?

With my beaming, solicitous groom at my side, I carried my train and bouquet from table to table, greeting and talking to my many relatives and friends who planted loving kisses on my rosy cheeks. Throughout the evening I flowed gaily among them, one and all, cameras catching me from every angle, until the smile frozen on my face began to fade. My feet hurt and my spirits flagged. My face grew flushed.

"Is everything all right, dear?" Bertram asked, speaking close to my ear.

"I'd like to sit down," I said. "And I think I need a drink."

"Certainly, my darling bride."

"I feel chilly, too. I'd like my wrap."

"It's quite warm, here, Carla. Too much excitement,

perhaps? Are you sure you're feeling well?"

"Of course, I'm sure," I snapped. "Would I ask if I wasn't?"

"Of course, dear. I'll get it for you if you tell me where it is."

"It's in the limousine. I left it on the seat."

"That's a bit of a distance. Rather than leave our guests, I'll send someone right down to fetch it."

"No. You can get it. I don't want anything to happen to it. It's valuable and I don't trust anyone else handling it." I slipped out of my shoes and flexed my cramped toes.

Bertram sighed. "All right, dear. It will only take a few minutes, anyway. I'll go down now and have someone bring your drink to you."

I felt pouty and didn't know why. Bertram couldn't be nicer and there I was, a twenty-five year old acting like a five-year-old spoiled brat. I didn't have to send him personally on the errand; I just didn't want to be fawned over and doted upon every other second. It irritated me. I was growing wearier by the minute and wished the night would end. At the same time I wished it would never end. I was afraid of what was coming. So afraid of losing my—

"The drink Mr. Kirby ordered for you, Mrs. Kirby," a server said, and handing it to me and moving away.

I sipped it. It tasted bitter, bitter as the thought of the honeymoon, the dreaded honeymoon in Aruba, and my heart sank. But why should it? I loved Bertram. He was my husband now. Why—

A disturbance erupted on the stairs. People milled around. Voices rose. A group of people rushed to my side, surrounding me, my father first among them. I stood up, spilling my drink, bewildered.

"Carly," he said, taking my glass, "don't be alarmed. There's been an accident."

"An accident?" I said, frantically looking past their faces. "What kind of accident?"

"It's Bertram. He's been hurt."

"Ber—How—what happened? Is it serious?"

"Here," my father called, "quickly, someone bring her a glass of water."

"No," I cried, stumbling over my gown, gathering it up and clutching it before rushing barefooted across the floor to the stairs. "Is it serious, tell me!"

Others followed behind me, trying to hold me back.

"Please, let me go," I said, fighting their hands, "let me go!"

They relented, but followed me down the staircase, pleading with me to return with them.

Outside, impervious to the stones cutting my feet, I raced across the parking lot into the street where a crowd had already collected around the limousine. They parted at my approach, and I fell to my knees beside Bertram's still form, crumpled on the pavement, my wrap in his hand. I called his name over and over, seeing the pool of blood, expanding almost imperceptibly in the near dark, seeping into the threads of my gown. I saw his eyes closed, his mouth open. I didn't want to believe it. "Bertram" I cried over and over, shaking him, "Bertram!" but I knew he was dead. I ripped the wrap from his hands and flung it away.

I screamed his name and finally collapsed. I remembered nothing until I woke up in one of the hotel rooms. When my eyes opened, I saw my parents hovering over me. "Mother…"

"It's all right, Carla," my mother said, standing beside me, stroking and caressing my forehead with her soft hand. "Just relax dear…"

"Mother…Bertram…is he…is he…?"

My father came close to me. "They've rushed him to the hospital, Carly. We'll have to wait to hear."

But I already knew.

"It's my fault, Daddy, my fault. If—"

"Hush, dear," my mother said, squeezing my hand. "Hush."

I couldn't face them and turned my head away. I couldn't help sobbing. "It should have been me, Mother, it should have been me."

My mother bent over to hug me. "Don't blame yourself, dear. It couldn't be helped. It was hit and run."
"Oh, Mother, if I hadn't…if only I hadn't…Oh, Mother, I wish I could die."

My father spoke. "Carly, that's nonsense. It's the Lord's will. I don't want to hear such words pass your lips. Everything will be all right, I promise."

"Carla, Doctor Epstein's here. He wants to give you something."

The doctor stepped in with a tablet and cup of water. "Take this, Carla. It will help."

My mother held the cup to my mouth.

I tried to speak, to explain, but the words wouldn't come. I grew drowsy. I slept…

Chapter 26

I knelt on the pavement of Sam's parking lot, my arms encircling Bryan, blinded by my tears and choking on the words I was trying to speak.

Bryan sat up slowly and glanced around. "It's okay, Carly, it's okay," he said, climbing to his feet and pulling me up with him. "See?" he said, extending his arms and slapping his sides, "one piece." He turned around like a dancer. "Look. Not a scratch."

"I thought...I thought..."

Bryan saw me trembling and pulled me into his arms. "It will take more than getting sideswiped by a car to get me out of your life."

"If anything had happened to you...if that car...I could never...never have...."

"Never have what, Carly?"

"I could never have lived through that again."

"Lived through what again? I don't understand."

"Oh, Bryan, didn't you ever wonder why I was in the cemetery the day we met?"

"No, Carly, I just assumed...to tell you the truth, I don't know what I assumed, if anything at all."

"I was there for my husband, Bertram. He was killed by a car on that date, the date of our wedding anniversary."

Bryan put his finger to my lips. "That's enough, Carly. If you want to, you can tell me another time. All I know is that if you hadn't shoved me away, I would've been under the wheels

244

of that Lexus instead of just being grazed by it. You saved my life, Carly."

"You mean I almost cost you your life."

He wiped a tear from my cheek with his thumb. "I don't know how you figure, but it's not your fault."

"If I didn't act like a…like a brat and force you to chase after me out of Sam's…"

"Well, brat, you know what this means, don't you?"

I looked at him, puzzled.

"Since you saved my life, you are now responsible for it." He smiled. "It's an old Chinese proverb. In short, you're never going to get rid of me."

"Bryan," I said, gazing up to him, "I love you. I love you so much. I've loved you since the moment our eyes first met but I was afraid. Do you understand? I was terribly afraid. Can you understand that?"

"Completely," he said, bringing his face close to mine. "And I've loved you since the moment I saw you standing there with your hair blowing in the wind and the autumn leaves twirling out of the trees and sprinkling down around you."

"I'm still afraid, Bryan. I'm afraid somehow I'll lose you, that something terrible will happen again."

He took me by the shoulders, his eyes locked onto mine. "Fate brought us together, Carly. And it will keep us together. It was meant to be. Nothing will ever separate us, not ever."

"I believe you, my darling, my love," I said, falling into his arms and wrapping my arms tight around him. "I do believe you. I do."

Brian held me close in his strong embrace as we gazed into

each other's eyes, knowing our love was permanent and real. He pressed his eager lips to mine. It was a kiss that promised to last a lifetime.

Epilogue

Bryan learned that Carly's marriage to Bertram Kirby III had been quickly annulled and, at Carly's insistence, no effort was made to profit financially from the tragedy in any way. Six months after the near fatal assault on Bryan's life by Cindy, he married Carly. As per Carly's wishes, the wedding was a small and intimate affair, with only the closest of family and friends attending. Among them were Lisa and Robbie as Best Man and Maid of Honor. The reception was catered by Sam and Katie in their restaurant, the Italian Garden.

Within the following six months, Bryan had submitted a restructuring plan for Miller Industries, which met SEC guidelines and in less than a year turned the company around. Unfortunately, Carly's father passed away, but not before seeing his daughter happily married and the company's fortunes on the rise.

Lisa and Robbie became engaged after Robbie's graduation, and were married a year later. Robbie landed a job teaching English in the local high school and continues to write poetry in his spare time. A publisher has shown some interest in his latest work. Lisa entered a weight loss program and graduated to become a fitness instructor. Their first child is expected next summer.

David was arrested and sentenced to three and a half to ten years in prison on various charges and for his assault on Lisa. After witnesses came forward to testify and Bryan asked for leniency, Cindy was given a suspended sentence, a ten thousand dollar fine and 500 hours of community service.

www.ingramcontent.com/pod-product-compliance
Lightning Source LLC
Chambersburg PA
CBHW050506260626
47157CB00004B/1204